MW01137985

# A Turn in Their *Dance*

## A Pride and Prejudice Variation

# Linda C. Thompson

Tales from Meryton - A Pride and Prejudice Short Story Collection
First Edition

Copyright © 2019 Linda C. Thompson
All Rights Reserved

For information, please contact:
Linda C. Thompson Books
1700 Lynhurst Lane
Denton, TX  76205

Cover Design: Lori Whitlock (www.loriwhitlock.com)
Cover Photo & Graphic Flourish:  Depositphotos.com
Photo By: @nejron
Flourish By:  @PinkPueblo

ISBN-13: 978-1-7332420-0-4
ISBN-10: 1-7332420-0-7

# DEDICATION

THIS BOOK IS DEDICATED TO ELIZABETH Ann West. Thank you for the guidance, encouragement, and support you gave me as I started down this path to becoming an author. Your friendship has been an added blessing.

This is also dedicated to the many phenomenal writers I have met along the way. I am in awe of your talents and amazed by your creativity. I also appreciate the other friendships that have developed. I could not have continued down this road without your inspiration and succor. There are too many of you to name, but I hope you know who you are and how much you are admired and appreciated.

# TABLE OF CONTENTS

# HARSH WORDS BEFORE UNDERSTANDING

With the exception of the family patriarch, every member of the Bennet family anxiously anticipated that night's assembly. As usual, gossip spread that the new resident of Netherfield Park would be in attendance with a large party of friends. The excitement was not limited to the Bennet household but, rather, felt by every eligible young lady in the neighborhood. Many a mother schemed for the best way to present her daughters to the wealthy young man who had recently taken up residence in their quiet country neighborhood.

The assembly room filled earlier than usual, as no one wished to miss the entrance of the new arrivals. As the clock struck eight o'clock in the evening, the dancing began despite the fact that the Bingley party had yet to make an appearance. The second dance of the set was underway when the turning dancers stopped in their tracks at the sight of the elegantly attired party standing in the doorway. As the music also stuttered to a stop, Sir William Lucas made his way to the entrance to greet the new arrivals. As the only titled gentleman in this part of Hertfordshire, he considered himself the official greeter of all newcomers. He waved to his family members as he passed, gathering them to him for an introduction.

"Mr. Bingley! Welcome, sir. We are delighted that you and your party could join us tonight." Sir William's words were directed toward a handsome young man of above average height whose face exhibited a large smile. He had reddish-blond hair that curled naturally, and his blue eyes shone like the summer sky.

"Good evening, Sir William. Please allow me to present the others of my party." Indicating a tall, slender young woman in a garish burnt orange gown with matching feathers in her hair, the man said, "This is my younger sister and hostess, Miss Caroline Bingley. Beside her is my elder sister, Mrs. Louisa Hurst, and her husband, Oliver Hurst." This time, Mr. Bingley indicated a short, plump woman in a blue gown. Though more pleasing in color, the gown – and its small owner – nearly drowned in frills and furbelows. Her husband appeared to be of a height with the younger woman and exhibited an obvious fondness for his food, as evidenced by the strain on the buttons of his waistcoat.

Behind the others stood perhaps the tallest and most attractive man Elizabeth Bennet had ever seen. His dark hair curled against his collar and on his brow. He wore black evening attire with a crisp white shirt and cravat. His white vest, shot through with green and silver threads, set off his elegantly-tied cravat in whose folds sat a large emerald stick pin that matched the color of his eyes. To Elizabeth's disappointment, those eyes stared above the heads of all those present and contained a look of disapproval. "Lastly, allow me to present my dearest friend, Fitzwilliam Darcy of Pemberley in Derbyshire."

The newcomers smiled politely as they were introduced to Sir William's family. As soon as the introductions were over, Miss Bingley and Mrs. Hurst moved to the side of the room, where they put their heads together and whispered behind their fans. Mr. Hurst made a beeline for the refreshment table. He filled a glass of punch and downed it before filling it a second time. Seeing an empty chair nearby, Mr. Hurst settled in for the evening. Mr. Darcy quietly followed Bingley for several minutes, listening to the introductions but saying almost nothing. They came to a party of six women, two of whom Darcy thought did not look old enough to be out. As he looked over the ladies, he was stunned when he encountered a pair of sparkling brown eyes in a face surrounded by delicate curls. He could not prevent himself from staring at the petite beauty, whose face held a question as she met his eyes.

Unfortunately, a shrill voice interrupted the moment, expressing the desire to know if Bingley had come intending to dance for the evening.

"Indeed, I have, Mrs. Bennet. In fact, Miss Bennet, if you are not engaged for the set that is forming, might I have this dance?"

"Thank you, Mr. Bingley. I should be pleased to dance with you." The voice that replied to Bingley's question was soft and silvery. Darcy turned to take in the speaker. What he saw was an extraordinarily beautiful young woman. Her features were delicate and she had the golden blond hair and blue eyes that society currently considered fashionable. She possessed an appearance of serenity that Darcy found lacking as compared to her more vibrant sister. Darcy watched as Bingley led the young woman—Miss Bennet was her name—to the dance floor.

Darcy was still observing his friend when that annoying voice again spoke. "I hope you have come to dance, Mr. Darcy, as has your friend. Any of my daughters would make you an excellent partner."

His natural shyness coming to the fore at the thought of addressing this matchmaking country matriarch, Darcy slipped his protective mask into place. "No thank you, madam, I do not care for dancing." So saying, Darcy turned on his heel and marched to the nearest corner, where he folded his arms across his chest and stared unseeing at the crowd around him.

With a feeling of disappointment, Elizabeth Bennet, the second eldest of the five Bennet daughters, watched him leave. Mr. Darcy was the most handsome man she had ever seen, and his voice when he spoke was deep and well-modulated. However, she found his haughty manners disturbing.

The evening passed as evenings usually did for the Bennet sisters. With the exception of Mary, the middle sister, they were all desirable as partners. Unfortunately, fewer gentlemen than usual were in attendance since it was harvest time. The evening was more than half over when Elizabeth found herself seated beside her sister, Mary, without a partner for the current set. Knowing it would do no good to interrupt Mary while she read, Elizabeth watched the dancers as her foot tapped along with the music. During the brief pause between the dances of one set, Mr. Bingley approached his friend.

"Come, Darcy. I must have you dance. Why do you insist on standing about in this silly fashion?"

"You know I do not care to dance unless I am particularly acquainted with my partner."

"Let me ask Miss Bennet to introduce you to one of her sisters. There is one sitting down just behind us."

Unaware that Elizabeth had taken a seat beside her younger sister, Mary, he did not turn to look. "She is not handsome enough to tempt me to dance, Bingley, nor am I in the mood to give consequence to young women who are slighted by other men. Return to your partner and enjoy her smiles."

"Is she not the most beautiful angel?" cried Bingley.

Darcy rolled his eyes.

"I would not be as fastidious as you for a kingdom. I shall return to my lovely partner and enjoy her company for as long as I may this evening. I do hope you will try harder in the future to make a better impression on my new neighbors than you are doing so far." With a chuckle, Bingley hurried away to rejoin Jane.

Though Darcy had not spoken loudly, Elizabeth had heard his harsh words. After Bingley's departure, Darcy took a step farther from the dance floor, bringing him closer to Elizabeth. Turning to Mary, Elizabeth raised her voice slightly. "I find it surprising that some people think themselves above their company. I always thought the sign of a true gentleman was that he treated everyone he met with respect or at least common courtesy. It is sad that Mr. Bingley's friend and family do not possess his good manners."

The softly spoken words reached Darcy's ears, causing him to blush deeply. He had not wished to attend the assembly that evening, as his worry for his dear sister, Georgiana, was all-consuming. Darcy recognized that he was not fit for company, but Miss Bingley's offer to remain at Netherfield with him was to be avoided at all costs. Darcy knew he should apologize, but he would need a moment or two to compose himself and order his thoughts. With that in mind, he skirted the room and made his way through the doors leading to the small balcony at the back of the building.

Having observed the gentleman's changing color, Elizabeth felt vindicated for his hurtful remarks. Her spirits improved, she went in search of her friend, Charlotte Lucas, to share her cleverness with the person who, after her sister Jane, was dearest to her.

While making her way around the room, Elizabeth reached the door to the balcony only to hear a hushed but anguished cry. As she paused to inquire if she could be of assistance, soft words from the darkness barely reached her ears. "Oh, dear sister, my sweet Georgie. How can you ever forgive me? I failed you. It never occurred to me that I would need to protect you from such a thing. To complicate matters, in all my worry, I have made a poor impression on Bingley's neighbors and insulted a lovely young woman."

Elizabeth gasped at the whispered words. The soft sound caused the anguished gentleman to whip around. Turning away would be rude, so Darcy looked down and brought his hand to the bridge of his nose, swiping at his eyes with his thumb and forefinger. Then, taking a deep breath, he looked up to meet the gaze of the young woman standing in the open doorway.

"Miss Elizabeth, please allow me to apologize for my earlier words. I am afraid my mood was not appropriate for an evening out, but I did not wish to disappoint Mr. Bingley. I arrived just this afternoon and am dealing with a family matter that makes me unsuitable for company. Wishing only to stop my friend's attempts at persuasion, I spoke without thought, not even glancing around to see of whom he spoke." Knowing he was rambling, Darcy clamped his jaws shut.

Elizabeth stared for a moment, unsure what to make of the gentleman before her. Mr. Darcy had originally appeared haughty and proud, but the man before her was both humble and seemingly broken. "Though I did not mean to eavesdrop, Mr. Darcy, your resonant voice carried some of what you said to my ears. I can easily understand that your concerns might make you wish for solitude rather than being forced to socialize. I am happy to accept your apology. If there is anything I can do to be of assistance to you or your sister, I hope you will not hesitate to contact me. A burden shared is a burden halved. I can assure you, I will keep your confidence if you need a listening ear."

"After my dreadful behavior, I do not deserve your forgiveness or assistance."

"Well, you have both. I will leave you to your thoughts, sir. I hope you can resolve the difficulties you are facing."

Elizabeth turned to go, but was brought up short by Darcy's call of, "Please, wait." She stopped and looked at him over her shoulder. "Might I ask how old your younger sisters are?"

Elizabeth was surprised by the question but answered without hesitation. "Lydia is five and ten, and Kitty is just seven and ten. May I ask how old your sister is?"

"Georgiana just turned six and ten. She is more than ten years my junior. I am her guardian, along with my cousin, Colonel Richard Fitzwilliam."

"Is your cousin also unmarried?"

Darcy stiffened at her words but nodded.

"I imagine that raising a young lady presents its challenges for two bachelors."

The tension left him as she finished speaking. "That is an understatement. My mother passed away when Georgiana was only two. Though I love my sister dearly and am happy to provide anything that will give her comfort or enjoyment, I am afraid that the experiences and challenges faced by a young woman are completely foreign to me."

Elizabeth noticed the music ending and realized they had been alone together for some time. "Mr. Darcy, my offer of support is sincere, but perhaps it is best if we find an equally quiet but more public place in which to speak. In such a small town, it does not take much to stir up gossip. I believe you carry enough to concern you at present and do not need to have the additional burden of being the source of gossip placed on you. I shall enter and make my way to my sister. If you wish to continue our discussion, you might ask Mr. Bingley to introduce us. I am engaged for the next two sets but am then available to dance or to continue our discussion."

"That is an excellent suggestion, Miss Elizabeth. I will join you shortly."

# MISS BINGLEY'S ANGER AND ANTAGONISM

CAROLINE BINGLEY'S ANNOYANCE WITH THE EVENING continued to mount. The inhabitants of this backwater village, nothing more than rustics, did not compose the kind of society to which she was accustomed. Even those members of the landed gentry in attendance left much to be desired. Adding to her disgust were the mediocre music and the ladies' fashions, which were at least two years out of style. To make matters worse, Mr. Darcy had not yet asked her for a dance. Her style and grace would stand out in such a setting, showing the gentleman from Derbyshire that she was an excellent choice for his wife and the mistress of his many homes. Caroline imagined herself filling Darcy House with dinners, musicales, and balls on a weekly basis. Of course, she would have to redecorate it from top to bottom. Though Lady Anne's lovely taste made for an elegant home, the house did not possess the style Caroline desired. Miss Bingley wanted there to be no doubt about her wealth. Since her years at the exclusive ladies seminary, she had been forced to deal with the snobbery of the ladies whose fathers held titles and land. The Bingley family had made their fortune in trade and Charles, though planning to purchase an estate, did not yet have a country house to call his own. Until he did, the worst of the denigration would continue.

As a result of the treatment she received from others, Caroline Bingley had developed a superior attitude toward those she considered beneath her. Unfortunately, she failed to remember that, despite her family's wealth, many of those upon whom she currently looked down were actually above her in society's eyes. At that moment, she noted Elizabeth Bennet returning to the room from the balcony. Caroline waited to learn whom the young woman had been meeting. What kind of swain would wish for such an unfashionable young lady for a wife?

Miss Bingley was in for a shock when, not five minutes later, Mr. Darcy entered the ballroom. Miss Bingley attempted to make her way through the crowd to the French doors where Mr. Darcy stood, but several of the matrons wished to make her acquaintance and learn more about the fashions in town as well as any other news they might garner. With frustration, Caroline observed her prey making his way across the room to the very young lady whose company he had enjoyed while on the balcony. Caroline Bingley watched in horror as the gentleman bowed over Elizabeth Bennet's hand as her brother introduced them. They continued to converse until a gentleman approached Miss Elizabeth and escorted her to the dance floor. Darcy, recalling Elizabeth's words on gentlemanly behavior, proceeded to ask Miss Mary Bennet and then Miss Charlotte Lucas to dance. Her eyes nearly popping from her head, she saw Darcy two confirmed wallflowers to dance. Miss Bingley's horror grew a she watched Mr. Darcy offer his arm and lead Miss Elizabeth to the set that was forming. Both wore smiles as they looked at each other. Mr. Darcy never smiled at her while they danced, nor did he make eye contact, always staring somewhere over her shoulder. Miss

Bingley struggled to understand the look that Mr. Darcy bestowed on the young woman before him. It showed both interest and something more that she could not quite decipher.

Just then, her attention was demanded by Mrs. Bennet, who paused beside Miss Bingley to watch the dancers. "They make a lovely couple, do they not?"

Her attention having been focused solely on Mr. Darcy and Elizabeth Bennet, Miss Bingley turned her head, planning to warn away this dreadful family by informing Mrs. Bennet that she and Mr. Darcy had almost come to an understanding. However, when she looked at the woman, it was to see her focused on a different couple in the line of dancers. With a small huff, Caroline realized her brother was dancing with Miss Jane Bennet for the second time that evening. Charles had barely left her side since their introduction. It would not do to insult her own brother, so with a forced smile and a clenched jaw, she ground out, "Indeed, they do."

Miss Bingley's words pleased Mrs. Bennet, who launched into a recitation of her eldest daughter's qualities. Her voice was a bit louder than necessary, and Miss Bingley knew that everyone around them heard Mrs. Bennet's words about what a lovely couple her daughter and Charles made. Caroline's night just kept getting worse.

As the music for the set began, Darcy realized the risk of being overheard. If they spoke of his sister's near ruin, it had the potential to destroy her reputation. Consequently, as the steps of the dance brought them close for the first time, Darcy attempted the small talk he so disliked.

"What activities are found in Meryton for visitors, Miss Elizabeth?

"The neighborhood contains several lovely walking trails, one of which leads to Oakham Mount, where you can enjoy an excellent view of the area in all directions. You will also find a well-stocked bookshop and a few skilled craftsmen who make unusual gifts. I might recommend some for your sister if you should be interested."

"Those all sound enjoyable and I would appreciate your assistance in finding a gift for my sister."

"Should you pay a call on Longbourn, a walk into Meryton might be arranged. I could show you the best options for a young lady." Noticing his eyebrows rise at her words, she blushed deeply and hurriedly added, "Or, perhaps, we should arrange a day and time to meet for me to do so. I do not expect you to call upon me."

"I suspect my friend will wish to pay his respects and I would not object to accompanying him." Darcy followed his utterance with a broad smile.

"Also, as the neighborhood is small, and with newcomers to our society, I would expect dinners, card parties, and teas with great frequency. Some in the neighborhood may even be inclined to hold a ball or two." Elizabeth saw the look of aversion that quickly crossed his face. Her annoyance rose again. Then, remembering the concerns she'd overheard, she said, "You need not worry, Mr. Darcy. You will find most of those you encounter to be pleasant." Elizabeth's tone was more clipped than she intended, as she felt his dislike of her friends and neighbors.

A quizzical look crossed his face at her tone. Darcy looked at his partner sharply. "Did I say something to offend you?"

She merely shook her head, not trusting her voice to reply.

The dance separated them and Darcy thought back over their conversation. It occurred to him that perhaps his dislike of such events showed on his face as she spoke. When the music brought them together again, he said, "Miss Elizabeth, may I tell you a secret?"

She looked at him askance but nodded.

"I suffer from shyness and always find myself unable to make conversation with those with whom I am not well acquainted."

"You do not seem to be having a difficult time talking to me. If you were to practice, you might overcome your discomfort."

"You have been graciousness itself after my less-than-pleasant words, but there is another facet to my discomfort in large gatherings."

"And what might that be, Mr. Darcy?"

"Did you by any chance hear discussion of my income and marital status before meeting myself or even Mr. Bingley?"

Elizabeth could not help the blush that covered her face. Unable to meet his eyes as they passed in the dance, she quietly replied, "I may have heard some mention of it."

"Can you imagine how it feels to know that your lineage and financial status are the main focus of people's interest in you? Would you enjoy being unable to discern whether someone's interest was in you the person or in your wealth and connections?"

"I doubt I would enjoy the sensation," Elizabeth answered. "My sister, Jane, and I have always stated that we would wed only for true affection and respect. Having to wonder what people liked about me would be very bothersome. But, as everyone in the neighborhood knows that my sisters and I possess very small dowries, I have not faced that issue. I do realize that I have only my charms to recommend me, and I doubt that I will ever find a sensible man who would accept me for so little. I imagine I shall spend my days as the doting aunt to my sister's children, teaching them to love nature and play the piano very ill."

Darcy was surprised at the honesty with which she spoke. He could not help a big smile at her reply. He found her straight-forward attitude refreshing. He also enjoyed her wit and found her very lovely. If he were honest with himself, he was enjoying this dance more than any other in memory. "I believe you exaggerate, Miss Elizabeth. I rather think that some intelligent gentleman might see you for your honesty, joyfulness, and generosity of spirit. If he were foolish enough to not recognize your good qualities because of a lack of connections or fortune, he would not be worthy of you." The smile that accompanied his words created a dimple in one cheek, the appearance of which mesmerized Elizabeth. "Do you often walk to Oakham Mount, I believe you called it?"

"Yes, I do. I prefer to start my morning with a walk. It helps me find a sense of peace that carries me through the day. Living with an excitable mother and three younger sisters with diverse personalities, it is the only peace I get in my day," said Elizabeth with a chuckle.

"Would you permit me to join you on one of your walks so that you can show me Oakham Mount?"

"Why, Mr. Darcy, I am surprised at you!" Elizabeth teased. "It would be highly inappropriate for me to make such an arrangement." Though Elizabeth's face showed a smile, Darcy flushed at the truth of her words. "However, should you happen to strike out on the path from Netherfield's back garden that leads to the southeast, there would be nothing improper in our accidentally happening upon each other."

Darcy's face brightened. "Indeed, there would not," he agreed with a matching smile. "Perhaps we will encounter one another there sometime soon."

"There is no better place from which to watch the sunrise than the summit of Oakham Mount." They smiled at one another before the steps of the dance separated them again. The dance ended shortly thereafter as they bowed and curtsied to each other.

As they began the second dance, Darcy remarked, "You mentioned the bookstore in Meryton. Are you fond of reading, Miss Elizabeth?"

"Indeed, I am, sir. My father has always allowed me the freedom to read anything in his library."

"What might be your favorite topic when reading?"

"I love poetry and Shakespeare. I also read history, philosophy, and agricultural journals. I convinced my father to try some of the new techniques regarding crop rotation."

"That is an unusual subject for a young lady." Darcy's look was thoughtful as he studied the lady before him. "What is your favorite play by Mr. Shakespeare?"

"I do not know if it is possible to pick just one. There is so much to admire in each of his works. I long to see one of them performed on the stage someday."

"Are you often in London?"

"I visit with my Aunt and Uncle Gardiner two or three times a year." She watched her partner closely as she said, "They reside near Cheapside."

Darcy was surprised to learn the location of her relatives' home, but did not let it show, asking only, "Is your uncle in trade?"

Her annoyance rising, Elizabeth bit out, "Yes, he is, Mr. Darcy, and you will not find a finer man. He is intelligent, kind, and successful."

"You sound very proud of him." Darcy's statement sounded more like a question.

"Yes, I am; he is a good man in every sense of the word. I do not believe that an accident of birth should define an individual. I prefer to judge a person on their behavior—not a title or status."

"I completely agree with you." At his words, Elizabeth studied his face, but his expression was open and honest. "I often encounter gentlemen of the ton who are hardly deserving of the title."

"I must say, Mr. Darcy, you surprise me. I would not have thought you so liberally-minded based on your earlier comments."

"I did apologize. Will you often remind me of my error?"

"Only if I believe you are behaving in such a way as to warrant a reminder," said Elizabeth with a broad smile.

As the set ended, Darcy escorted Elizabeth to the refreshment table for a cool drink.

Caroline Bingley kept a close eye on Mr. Darcy as he danced with Elizabeth Bennet. She slowly moved around the room so that she would be close to him when the set finished. Unfortunately, Mr. Darcy moved in the other direction, with Elizabeth Bennet still on his arm. Caroline followed their progress as they moved towards the refreshment table before quickly trailing the couple. As she caught up to her prey, she remembered her brother's seeming fascination with another of the Bennet sisters. Thus, she sought a way to end their evening. Just before reaching the couple, Caroline saw Darcy holding two glasses of punch. She pretended to stumble and put out her arms, shoving Mr. Darcy in the back.

Jostled from behind, Darcy, with horror in his eyes, could not prevent the punch from flying out of the glasses and dousing Elizabeth Bennet's face and gown. Shifting the empty glasses to one hand, he reached for his handkerchief and offered it to Elizabeth while tendering his apologies.

"Miss Bennet, please forgive me—" he began before a shrill voice cried out and a boney hand clutched his arm.

"Oh, Mr. Darcy, you saved me from injury. One of the local clods tripped me, nearly causing me to crash to the floor. How wonderful you are!" Darcy shook off the arm and ignored the woman now standing beside him as he attempted to offer Elizabeth further assistance. Caroline turned her attention on Elizabeth as she dried her face and wiped at the moisture on her gown. "Oh, Miss Eliza, you are here too." Caroline looked at the ruined gown and smiled with mock sympathy. "You appear to have ruined your dress; you must be more careful when drinking in such a crowded room. What a shame that you and your family shall have to depart early." Her self-satisfied smirk was evident to all those who stood nearby. Darcy looked concerned that he had caused the ruin of one of Elizabeth's gowns.

Elizabeth, who had noticed Miss Bingley's progress across the room, calmly replied, "And you must learn to watch where you are walking in such a crowded room; you appeared to trip over your own feet just before bumping into Mr. Darcy."

Those of her friends standing nearby snickered at Elizabeth's words. Others grumbled at Miss Bingley's insult, saying, "There was no one near her."

"It will not be necessary for my family to depart," Elizabeth continued. "I will ask the coachman to take me home and return for my family. I would not wish to curtail their enjoyment of the evening."

"Please, Miss Elizabeth, allow me to escort you home since the accident was my fault. Perhaps Miss Mary, who is sitting just over there, would accompany us to provide proper chaperonage."

"But, Mr. Darcy, you would put yourself at risk of this woman compromising you!" blustered Miss Bingley.

Darcy turned such a withering look on Caroline that she took a step back. "As a gentleman, it is my responsibility and pleasure to offer my assistance."

Elizabeth hesitated but a moment before nodding. Charlotte, who had been approaching to speak with Elizabeth, had observed the entire scene. She offered to fetch Mary and inform Mrs. Bennet of the incident."

Elizabeth looked panicked for a moment. Her expression must have alerted Charlotte as to her misgivings, for with a small nod she moved away in the direction of Mary.

Darcy offered Elizabeth his arm and escorted her around the edge of the room, shielding her from view to the best of his ability. They moved into the entry hall. Once there, Darcy requested a servant to fetch both Miss Elizabeth's and Miss Mary's cloaks. He finished assisting Elizabeth with her outerwear as Mary arrived.

"Are you well, Lizzy?" asked Mary as Mr. Darcy helped her, as well, with her cloak.

"Yes, Mary, just a little damp. Thank you for accompanying us. Mr. Darcy kindly offered to take me home so that Mama and Jane could continue to enjoy the evening."

Mary did not reply. She followed Mr. Darcy and Elizabeth into the darkness.

# MR. DARCY'S OFFER

MR. DARCY CALLED FOR BINGLEY'S COACH and took the ladies to Longbourn. While Mrs. Hill assisted Elizabeth up the stairs, Mr. Hill led Mr. Darcy to Mr. Bennet's bookroom.

Mr. Bennet started at the knock on the study door. Looking at the mantle clock, he wondered who would disturb him at such an hour but he quickly called, "Come."

Opening the door, Mr. Hill announced, "Mr. Darcy to see you, sir."

Mr. Bennet looked confused but nodded at Mr. Hill to admit the man.

Upon entering, Darcy bowed and said, "Excuse me for disturbing you so late, sir. My name is Fitzwilliam Darcy. I am a guest of Mr. Bingley's at Netherfield Park."

"How do you do, Mr. Darcy? How may I be of service?"

"It is I who hope to be of service to you, sir. I just brought Miss Elizabeth home after a minor mishap. Miss Mary accompanied her sister."

"Is my Lizzy well?"

"Yes, sir. However, as I was retrieving a drink for her after our dance, someone bumped against me quite forcefully and the drinks spilled on Miss Elizabeth. The stain will ruin the dress. I would beg your permission, Mr. Bennet, to replace the damaged gown. I know it is an unusual request and that such a gift would normally be permissible only by a betrothed. However, I would be happy to purchase something and allow you to present it, sir. No one need know of my involvement—even Miss Elizabeth."

Mr. Bennet studied the man before him for some time before speaking. "It is not necessary for you to do this, Mr. Darcy. I can afford to purchase dresses for my daughters."

"I mean no offense, Mr. Bennet. It is obvious that you take good care of your daughters' needs. However, my conscience requires me to replace the gown which was damaged at my hand."

Again, Mr. Bennet stared at the gentleman before him. He could not figure out what interest the man had in his Lizzy. What would compel him to make such a gesture? Darcy began to shift slightly under the pressure of Mr. Bennet's stare before the gentleman finally spoke. "It seems you will not be dissuaded." Darcy shook his head. "Then I will permit you to replace Lizzy's dress. Just request that Mrs. Harris send the dress to me upon completion."

Darcy hesitated before speaking further. "Were I to place the order, Mr. Bennet, it would call your daughter's reputation into question. Perhaps it would be best if the order came from you. I could tell you what I wish to purchase for her or write it out for you to sign."

Thomas Bennet sighed at the further delay in returning to his book but appreciated the gentleman's consideration of his Lizzy. "Very well, Mr. Darcy." Mr. Bennet pulled a sheet of parchment from a drawer and pushed it across the desk to the younger man. Mr. Darcy dipped the quill into the inkstand and began to write, pausing only briefly to consider his words. Elizabeth's face flashed in his mind's eye as he thought about which color gown to request. Her creamy skin and dark hair would be beautiful in pale yellow, but then he remembered the blush he had frequently seen on her cheeks. He thought a soft rose might also be becoming.

*12 October 1811*
*Longbourn*

*Dear Mrs. Harris,*

> *Please make an evening gown for Miss Elizabeth Bennet of pale yellow or soft rose silk, trimmed in the finest, most delicate lace you have in your shop. You are familiar with her preferred style. Send the gown and bill to Longbourn upon its completion. I will pay a five-pound bonus if you finish the dress within a week's time.*

*Sincerely,*

Darcy blew on the ink to dry it before handing the letter to Mr. Bennet for his signature. The gentleman did not even read it over before signing it. He folded the note and sealed it. "I will have this delivered first thing in the morning."

"Thank you, sir, for allowing me to do this for Miss Elizabeth. Please notify me when the bill comes and I will provide you the funds to pay it. "

"Yes, yes," said Mr. Bennet absently. He had already returned to the description of the Battle of Trafalgar he was reading.

Darcy bowed and exited the office. Mr. Hill waited in the hallway to show the gentleman to the door. Darcy mounted the carriage and returned to the assembly hall. Carriages lined up at the door, waiting to pick up passengers. He saw Bingley standing with the Bennet family, while his family stood to the side. Miss Bingley's lips were pressed tightly into a thin line and her foot tapped impatiently beneath the hem of her gown. Bingley noted his carriage passing and joining the end of the queue. Darcy stepped down and moved in the direction of his friend while Jane and Bingley moved toward him.

As soon as he was close enough to speak without being overheard, Jane Bennet's anxious voice softly asked, "How is Elizabeth, Mr. Darcy? Charlotte informed us that she was required to leave and that you kindly escorted her and Mary home."

"She is well, Miss Bennet. It was nothing serious. Unfortunately, punch spilled all over her, and she was wet and uncomfortable." As he spoke, Darcy glared at Caroline Bingley, who was staring at the threesome. Bingley noted his expression and wondered at whom he was scowling. He started to ask, but Darcy shook his head to forestall Charles' question.

At that moment, the Bennet carriage arrived at the front of the queue. Mr. Darcy remained where he was as Bingley escorted Jane to her carriage and assisted her in. Bingley watched for a moment as it pulled into the darkness. Then he returned to his friend.

"If it made you angry, why did you escort the ladies home, Darcy?"

"What do you mean, Bingley?"

"You were glaring into the distance as you spoke to Miss Bennet. I hope she did not notice your expression."

"I was not glaring into the darkness; I was glaring at your sister."

Bingley started at the anger in his voice, but then, with a resigned sigh, said, "What did Caroline do now?"

"She deliberately shoved me when I was holding two cups of punch. They spilled all over Miss Elizabeth, dowsing her and completely ruining her gown."

"Are you sure it was not an accident?"

"If you mean did I see her? No. However, her comments about the family having to go home were clear enough, as were the comments from those standing close enough to observe the incident."

Bingley shook his head. "Her dress was ruined?"

"Caroline said it was, with a rather gleeful expression."

"Well, then, I will have Louisa order a new one and deduct the cost from Caroline's allowance."

"I do not believe that is necessary. Besides, I do not think Mrs. Hurst and Miss Elizabeth have similar taste. If Miss Bingley gave her input, I am sure they would choose something that would only embarrass Miss Elizabeth."

"You may be right there," agreed Charles.

The Bingley carriage moved past them. The gentlemen stood behind the others of the party, allowing Mr. Hurst to assist the two women into the carriage. Darcy and Charles sat opposite the others as the vehicle pulled away.

"What a dreadful neighborhood you selected, Charles," came Miss Bingley's whiney voice.

"I do not know what you mean, Caroline. I found the company to be quite welcoming and friendly."

"Hardly, Charles. I am sure that Mr. Darcy would agree with me."

Darcy turned from the window to glare at her for bringing him into the conversation. He did not hesitate to agree with Charles before turning to stare out the carriage window again.

Caroline frowned at Darcy's response but did not speak for the remainder of the ride to Netherfield.

# A VISIT TO LONGBOURN

DARCY BEGAN THE NEXT DAY WITH a brisk morning ride across the sparkling fields around Netherfield. He noted what, in the distance, appeared to be the most significant hill in the area. As he studied the view around him, Darcy saw a form standing at the edge, silhouetted by the sunrise. A sudden gust of wind whipped her skirts around her, outlining her beautiful shape and blowing a mass of curls behind her. Mesmerized by the sight, Darcy could not help but wonder if it might be Miss Elizabeth, as the mount appeared to be located between Netherfield and Longbourn. He was thoughtful as he rode back to Netherfield. The evening he'd shared with Miss Bennet was unlike any experience he could recall in a ballroom.

Darcy's thoughts were abruptly interrupted upon his approach of the breakfast room, as the sound of Miss Bingley's grating voice reached his ears. Darcy frowned when he realized that she was continuing her complaints about the previous evening. He entered quietly, without acknowledging anyone, and filled a plate from the sideboard before sitting next to Charles. In the background, Miss Bingley's words droned on like the annoying buzz of an insect.

"Really, Charles, there is no one in this backward community of our level of society. The men barely deserve to be called gentlemen. The ladies' fashions are at least two years out of date. The music was dreadful and the dancing no better than that of the savages in Africa." Darcy and Bingley looked at one another and rolled their eyes at her turn of phrase. "I think you should close the house immediately. We should return to town before any of our acquaintances discover us in such an unfashionable locale. It may damage our acceptance in the ton."

As Caroline's complaints had begun the moment he had sat down to break his fast some thirty minutes earlier, Charles grumpily spoke when she paused for breath. "Caroline, if you wish to return to town, please do so with my blessing. I, however, will be staying right here. I leased this property with the intention of learning to manage an estate of my own, just as our father wished. If you choose to not return to town, I insist that you cease with these complaints forthwith. I may wish to entertain my neighbors at some point in the future and I will not risk you insulting them. If you do not feel up to the task, I shall ask Louisa to be my hostess. Which do you choose?"

As her brother spoke, several shades of red passed through Miss Bingley's face. "But Charles—"

"No buts, Caroline. Do you wish to return to London, or will you cease your criticisms of our neighbors and act as my hostess?"

Miss Bingley glared at her brother as she deliberated, then turned a look of loathing on Mr. Hurst as she heard him chuckle. He only laughed harder.

"I am waiting, Caroline."

"I shall be happy to remain as your hostess, Charles. Miss Jane Bennet seemed like a pleasant young lady; perhaps if I cultivate her friendship, I will better enjoy my time in Hertfordshire." The words were forced out between grated teeth and the downturn of her lips gave the lie to those words. Bingley decided to accept her word for now, but knowing his sister as he did, he suspected this would not be their last conversation on the topic.

Darcy, who had stayed silent throughout the conversation between the siblings, spoke. "Bingley, why do you not show me around the estate this morning, so that I can see if there are areas that need improvement?"

"That is an excellent idea, Darcy. How long before you can be ready?"

"Will fifteen minutes be soon enough?"

"I shall meet you at the stables." At that, the two men departed the room while Miss Bingley stared after them.

Arriving back at the house at half past one, the gentlemen requested trays in their rooms as they cleaned up in preparation of paying a call on Longbourn.

Having just argued with her younger sister, Kitty flounced away from the table where they sat retrimming their bonnets. She stared out the window, her arms folded across her chest and a pout on her face. Suddenly, Kitty emitted a small squeak that turned into a coughing fit.

"Really, Kitty, must you cough so? You know how it affects my nerves."

Coughing her last, Kitty said, "But, Mama, two men on horses are coming up the drive."

Lydia and Mrs. Bennet both squealed as they rushed to the window. Lydia pushed her sister out of the way to get a better view.

"Oh, Jane, I knew you could not be so beautiful for nothing. It is Mr. Bingley, and Mr.

Darcy appears to accompany him. He was so rude at the assembly, but if he is Mr. Bingley's friend, we shall have to tolerate him."

"Mama!" cried Jane.

"He danced with me, Mama," added Mary.

"Mr. Darcy is just shy in new company, Mama." Elizabeth's voice was the loudest in the gentleman's defense.

"Do not be ridiculous, Lizzy! Why would a man such as Mr. Darcy be shy when he is so rich?" Elizabeth shook her head at her mother's reasoning. "Quick, girls, tidy up the room before the gentlemen enter. Kitty and Lydia, return to your table. Mary, you and Elizabeth sit on the larger sofa. Jane, you sit on the small sofa. I will encourage Mr. Bingley to sit beside you."

"Mama, please do not push the gentleman towards me. I should prefer it to be his choice." Mrs. Bennet frowned and looked as though she would speak again, but Jane quickly continued. "Besides, you would not wish to frighten him away." Mrs. Bennet did not have time to reply, as Mr. Hill appeared in the doorway.

The girls scrambled to take their seats as Mr. Hill announced, "Mr. Bingley and Mr. Darcy." Mr. Hill moved aside to allow the gentlemen to enter.

"Good afternoon, Mr. Bingley, Mr. Darcy. How lovely to see you again," gushed Mrs. Bennet, though her tone was a bit cold when she spoke the second gentleman's name. Elizabeth blushed at her mother's rudeness. However, the worse was to come as her mother continued. "Does not my Jane look lovely today? Why do you not sit beside her, Mr. Bingley?" Now Jane, too, was blushing, but Mr. Bingley moved with alacrity to sit beside her.

Before Mrs. Bennet could further embarrass her daughters, Darcy seated himself in a chair beside the sofa on which Miss Elizabeth sat. He smiled in her direction, but she failed to observe it, as her eyes were cast down at the hands folded in her lap. Mrs. Bennet began to badger Bingley with questions that prevented him enjoying the quiet conversation he hoped to have with Miss Bennet. Fortunately, this left Darcy and Elizabeth free to converse uninterrupted.

Darcy spoke quietly. "How are you today, Miss Elizabeth? I hope no worse for the misfortune that befell you last evening."

Elizabeth looked up at his gentle voice and gave him a timid smile. "I am well, sir, I thank you. Did you wish to walk today and discuss your sister or would you prefer to go into Meryton and look for a gift for her?"

Darcy thought for a moment as he studied Elizabeth's upturned face. There was still a hint of embarrassment in her eyes, but her smile grew more confident.

"Perhaps we should remain here this afternoon. I should endeavor to improve your mother's impression of me."

Elizabeth blushed at his words. "If you wish."

"May I ask you a question, Miss Elizabeth?" She nodded. "Did you enjoy your walk to Oakham Mount this morning?"

Startled at Darcy's question, she blurted, "How did you know I walked there this morning?"

"I was out riding and you made a lovely silhouette against the beautiful sunrise." Elizabeth flushed at his words, and Darcy smiled widely.

Abruptly, their conversation was interrupted by Mrs. Bennet's shrill voice. "Tell us about your estate, Mr. Darcy. It is in Derbyshire, is it not?"

"Yes, madam. It is a largish estate near the Peak District. Along with the crops, we raise sheep and breed horses. It is near the town of Lambton."

"Lambton?" questioned Elizabeth. Darcy nodded. "My Aunt Gardiner grew up in that village and often speaks of it with fond memories."

"Is Gardiner her married name? Do you recall her maiden name? Perhaps I am acquainted with her family."

"It was Thompson. Her father still owns the bookshop there."

"Mr. Thompson is well known to me, as I am a frequent customer of his."

At that moment, Mrs. Hill appeared with the tea tray, which was loaded with scones, jam, and fresh clotted cream. "Jane, will you serve please?" asked her mother. Mr. Bingley could not take his eyes from her graceful actions as she went about her task.

Once Jane had served everyone, Darcy again spoke to Elizabeth. "Might you be induced to show me Oakham Mount tomorrow morning? I believe the privacy to be found there might be the perfect place for me to discuss my sister with you."

"I would be delighted to show you one of the most beautiful locations in the area. Do you remember which path to take from Netherfield?" Darcy answered with a nod. "Provided the weather cooperates, I will leave about 6:30. I should be at the spot where the paths meet by 6:50. That will allow us to reach the summit before the sun rises, if that suits you?"

"That sounds delightful. Is the path longer from Netherfield?"

"A little bit, but with your long strides, you should be able to cover the distance in about the same amount of time."

At that moment, Mr. Bingley rose to take his leave. "Thank you for the tea and company this morning, ladies. It was delightful to see you again." Though he spoke to all those in attendance, his eyes never left Jane's face.

"Jane, you and Lizzy walk the gentlemen to the door." The ladies both blushed at their mother's obviousness but rose to do as she requested.

At the door, Mr. Bingley bowed over Jane's hand, stopping just short of kissing it. Darcy followed suit, but he kept his eyes on Elizabeth and softly said, "Until tomorrow."

# SECRETS SHARED ON OAKHAM MOUNT

EXCITED FOR THE OPPORTUNITY TO MEET with Mr. Darcy, Elizabeth awoke early the next morning. In the kitchen, she pilfered two rolls that she filled with small slices of ham before wrapping them and putting them in her pocket. Elizabeth also grabbed two apples before escaping the house and making for the path to Oakham Mount.

Despite the fact that she'd arisen early, Mr. Darcy was waiting for her when she arrived at the spot where the paths converged. The gentleman removed his hat and made a sweeping bow.

"Good morning, Miss Elizabeth. How are you on this fine day?"

"Good morning to you as well, Mr. Darcy. I am well, thank you, and you?"

"I am hale and hardy. Shall we begin our climb?" asked Mr. Darcy as he offered his arm.

Elizabeth placed her hand in the crook of his arm and turned him towards the path that climbed up Oakham Mount. They ascended the steep trail in silence, but when they reached the summit, Elizabeth led the gentleman to a large, flat rock. Taking her seat, she waved at Mr. Darcy to do the same. Once he sat beside her, she pulled the cloth from her pocket and offered one of the rolls and one of the apples to her companion.

Quietly chewing the bite she had taken, Elizabeth waited for Darcy to begin. When he did not, she said, "As we were both early to the meeting point this morning, there is time for you to tell me more about your sister before the beauty of the day distracts us."

Darcy sat, thoughtful, as he swallowed the bite in his mouth. "I believe I must give you some background before I speak of Georgiana's current difficulties." Elizabeth nodded her consent and kept her eyes on the gentleman beside her. "My father, who passed away five years ago, was an excellent master and father. He had a dedicated steward named Mr. Wickham. Mr. Wickham had a son, George, who is near my age. As children, we were the best of friends. The elder Mr. Wickham died when George was ten and four, so my father, who was George's godfather, sent him to school with me and then later to Cambridge when I began my studies at university.

"During our time at school, I began to notice a change in George. You see, at Pemberley, he considered himself my equal. However, at school, the other students saw him only as the son of a servant. He did not receive the acceptance I did." Elizabeth gave another nod but did not interrupt as she continued to study the handsome face before her. "I tried my best to include George, but he became bitter and eventually fell in with a crowd that constantly got into trouble–though most of it seemed harmless while we were at Eton. However, by the time we reached university, his presence had become intolerable."

Again, Elizabeth nodded. The topic was obviously difficult for Darcy to discuss, so she maintained her silence.

"George Wickham's behavior at university is not appropriate for a gentlewoman's ears, but suffice it to say that he began to live a more dissolute lifestyle. I used my allowance to clean up after George. However, due to illness, I could not bring myself to disillusion my father about his cherished godson.

"When my father passed away, he left George a gift of one thousand pounds and a living in the church when it became available and provided that George took orders. Wickham told me he did not desire to be ordained and preferred to study the law. I must admit my relief, for he was certainly not someone who should watch over the spiritual welfare of anyone. I had some papers prepared and paid him three thousand pounds, in addition to the one thousand my father had gifted him. By signing the paperwork, he resigned all rights to the living.

"Two years later, the living became available and Wickham contacted me, demanding to receive it. I reminded him of the funds he had accepted in exchange for any claim on the position. He railed at me, telling me the seriousness of his position. Apparently, he had frittered away almost all of the four thousand pounds and now had debts in excess of his remaining funds. However, I remained firm in my refusal.

"Since that time, I know not how he lived, but the rumors he spreads wherever he goes often reach my ears. You see, he tells a very different version of the events surrounding the living. He claims that I denied it to him. Then, a few months ago, he reentered my life in a most despicable manner." Darcy paused to breathe deeply several times before he forced himself to continue. Though she did not speak, Elizabeth reached out her hand to cover his beside her on the rock. She squeezed his fingers gently before removing her hand and giving him an encouraging smile.

"This past summer, I removed Georgiana from school and, in company with her companion, took a house for her in Ramsgate to allow her to study with a painting master. After I left her there, George Wickham appeared. He dedicated himself to gaining her affection. Georgiana did not know about the break in our friendship, for it did not seem appropriate to subject her to a summary of Wickham's misdeeds. Between Wickham and her companion, Georgiana soon believed that she was in love with him. They pressured her to elope with Wickham. I discovered that George had a past connection to Mrs. Younge, Georgiana's companion."

A gasp escaped Elizabeth's lips. "Oh, your poor sister! Were you able to prevent her elopement, or is she doomed to a marriage with such a monster?"

Pleased at her reaction and concern for his sister, Darcy now covered her hand and squeezed it as he said, "Yes, I returned to Ramsgate earlier than expected and Georgiana confessed everything. Being the last of the Darcys, we have always had a close connection and she did not wish to disappoint such a beloved relation."

"Thank goodness for that! Please forgive my interruption and continue your tale."

Darcy smiled wearily. "As I said, I arrived early and found her in the parlor alone with Wickham. She indicated that Mrs. Younge, her companion at the time, would return momentarily. Several minutes passed but the companion did not return. I did not speak while we waited; I only stared at Wickham. I assume that my lack of speech unnerved Georgiana, for she jumped up and rushed into my arms, exclaiming, "I am so glad you arrived, William. Now we will not need to elope and you can give me away when I wed your dearest friend, George.'

"I was flabbergasted at the news and I glared at Wickham over my sister's head. I sent her in search of Mrs. Young, to give me the privacy I needed to confront Wickham. As soon as the sound of her footsteps faded away, I wheeled on George and came to tower over him where he sat. I enjoyed the next part of this experience, for I knew something of which George was not cognizant. Though I never felt equal to telling my father of Wickham's bad behavior, I convince him that I had observed enough such behavior at school to give me pause. I suggested that he add a clause to his will that required the approval of her guardians before Georgiana married and that her dowry would be forfeit if she wed without their consent. The look on Wickham's face when he heard this almost made up for the pain he had caused over the years. After hearing my explanation, he pushed me backward and rose from his seat. 'It appears you win this time, Fitzwilliam, but one day I will get my revenge,' Wickham drawled.

"'I would not count on it, for if you come near my family or me ever again, or if you say one word of this and cause harm to Georgiana's reputation, I will call your debts due and have you sent to Newgate for the remainder of your miserable life. I have cleaned up after you for years. The debts you owe are now more than three thousand pounds.'

"Wickham had blanched briefly before a mean look came over his face. 'Without her dowry, who would want such a dull, mealy-mouthed little girl for a wife? Come, Harriet, the game is up. Now we do not need to wait for this baby to be asleep before we can enjoy ourselves.'

"Unknown to me, Georgiana had returned and was standing in the doorway. You can imagine how she felt to hear the man she loved dismiss her with such unkind words. She sank to the floor in tears as Wickham walked past her and out of the house."

"Poor Georgiana," Elizabeth cried. "I take it your concern is in large part due to the fact that she has not recovered her spirits since that time?"

"Indeed, that is part of my poor mood. The other is my guilt at failing to protect my dear sister."

"Your guilt does neither you nor Georgiana any good. If she is aware that you feel guilty, it will only add to the burden of guilt she carries. You could not have anticipated his behaving in such a fashion, and you were correct in not exposing your innocent sister to such degenerate behavior."

"But what can I do to help her move past this? I do not like feeling so helpless. It frustrates me and causes me to behave poorly, as I did at the assembly the other evening."

"I can understand your frustration, but you must keep it hidden from your sister if you do not wish to add to her current cares. Is there a female in your family to whom Georgiana can talk?"

"Yes, there is a new companion, Mrs. Annesley. Georgiana is also close to my aunt, Lady Fitzwilliam."

Head cocked to the side, Elizabeth considered this information. "Are there any younger women or friends with whom she could

40

talk? Georgiana may feel that these ladies are too old to understand her feelings."

"There is, unfortunately, no one else. There is one female cousin who is just slightly younger than me. Though Anne would undoubtedly keep her secret, her mother, Lady Catherine, would not be so considerate of Georgiana. She would rail at her for her mistakes, leaving Georgie more damaged than she already is. Lady Catherine is also insistent that I marry her daughter. Though neither Anne nor I wish it, my aunt would post the marriage announcement should I show any attention to my cousin."

Elizabeth turned to look out at the horizon as she thought. She noticed that the sun was just beginning to rise. The area where the horizon met the sky was alight with colors. The edge of the sun appeared, a golden halo around it. As the colors climbed higher, the clouds seemed to turn orange, then pink. The sky above them, though still dark, showed the shape of the clouds against it as the background began to lighten. Brighter rays fanned out behind the clouds, lightening the darkness further. Elizabeth called her companion's attention to the sight as she continued to think of a solution. They sat in silence, taking in the magnificence of the scene before them.

Finally, Elizabeth spoke. "Do you believe your Aunt Fitzwilliam would be able to convince Lady Catherine to allow Anne to visit her? Perhaps she and Georgiana might meet in her home, thereby not encouraging your aunt in her delusions of a marriage."

Now it was Darcy's turn to sit in silent contemplation. "That might be possible, but Anne's health—though not as bad as her mother believes—is somewhat delicate. It might not be in her best interest to travel at this time of year. Also, I do not think Georgiana can wait until spring before unburdening herself."

"Oh," said Elizabeth. She once more turned her attention to solving this dilemma. "Do you think that if you were to write to Georgiana about my sisters and myself, she might wish to correspond with me? Perhaps during the course of our correspondence, she would open up to me."

Darcy considered this for some time. "I would be happy to write to her about you, but I am not sure she would have the courage to write to a stranger. The events at Ramsgate have exacerbated Georgie's natural shyness."

"Do you believe it would help her to join you at Netherfield?"

"Were Miss Bingley not in residence, I would say yes. However, Miss Bingley always intimidates Georgiana with her overly solicitous behavior and pretense of a close friendship."

"Yes, I could see how Miss Bingley's company would have the reverse effect on your sister. Elizabeth could not help the giggle that escaped her at the thought of Mr. Bingley's single sister.

"I will write to Georgie today and tell her more of you and your nearest sisters. If I make it sound interesting enough, perhaps she will ask about corresponding or visiting, despite Miss Bingley. I am sure that between lessons with her companion and visits with you, we can keep her away from Miss Bingley much of the time."

Elizabeth nodded in agreement. "I am sure we can. Perhaps you should wait to send your letter until you have a gift to send along with it."

"No, I believe I will write to her today of the events of last evening. My dancing at an assembly should be quite surprising enough to Georgiana." Darcy looked at the height of the sun in the sky and knew they had been alone for quite some time. "I believe it is time to depart, Miss Elizabeth. However, perhaps we could venture into Meryton on Tuesday to select a gift for my sister."

"I would be delighted to accompany you."

"Perhaps we should ask your sisters to come as well, as Miss Katherine and Miss Lydia bookend my sister in age. They may also have some good suggestions to make."

Elizabeth's musical laughter trilled on the morning air. "I believe you might find their help a little overwhelming, sir."

"You may be right, but perhaps a little attention from a gentleman of means will help them to calm and grow up a bit."

"It shall be as you wish. I promise not to say 'I told you so' should I be correct," said Elizabeth with another laugh.

Mr. Darcy again offered his arm as they descended the hill. At the point where the paths merged, Darcy bowed over Elizabeth's hand. "I thank you, Miss Elizabeth, for the lovely morning and the breakfast. I look forward to seeing you in church tomorrow." He remained still and watched until Elizabeth disappeared. Just before she passed from view, she turned and waved at him, then continued to her home. Darcy was contemplative as his long strides carried him back to Netherfield.

# A LETTER FOR MISS DARCY

GEORGIANA DARCY SAT AT THE PIANOFORTE in the music room, practicing the most recent piece from her music master. The melody was slow and melancholy, which exactly matched her mood. Mrs. Annesley, her new companion, sat in a chair by the window, attending to some needlework. Her eyes often strayed from the work in her hands to the young lady at the instrument. Though she was aware of Miss Darcy's recent experiences, she had not been able to break through the young woman's reserve to discuss the situation and offer suggestions. She did not wish to force the conversation but wondered if it would be necessary in order to assist her charge in better understanding what had occurred, as well as to help her learn from the experience. Perhaps she would consult Mr. Darcy for his opinion.

At a brief knock on the open doorframe, Georgiana paused in her playing. She looked up to observe Pemberley's housekeeper, Mrs. Reynolds, standing with a letter in her hand. "Excuse me for interrupting, Miss Georgiana, but you wished to know as soon as a letter arrived from your brother."

A smile lit Georgiana's face. She stood and rushed to take the letter from the small, smiling woman. "Thank you so much, Mrs. Reynolds. I did not expect to hear from William quite so soon, but I am very pleased to receive a letter." Looking at her companion, Georgiana asked, "May I be excused to read my letter? I promise to finish my practicing very soon." Mrs. Annesley nodded her acquiescence and Mrs. Reynolds stepped aside as the young woman rushed from the room. The two women shared a knowing look before the housekeeper returned to her duties.

Settled in the window seat of her bedchamber, Georgiana paused to study the Darcy crest in the sealed wax. She had come very near to disgracing the family name, which, though untitled, had long been respected throughout the country. She forced back the tears that threatened to fall and carefully broke the seal. Then she unfolded the letter and began to read.

*Netherfield Park*
*Hertfordshire*
*20 October 1811*

*Dearest Georgie,*

*I hope this letter finds you well and your spirits improving. Please be assured of my love for you and please accept that you did not do anything wrong. The fault lies with me for leaving you vulnerable to men such as Mr. Wickham.*

*However, I do not wish to dwell on the sadness of the recent past. Instead, I want to share with you some of my experiences with Mr. Bingley and his family. The estate that Bingley is leasing is of medium-size and very attractive. The fields around the estate are flat as far as the eye can see. The autumn colors are still riotous and give beauty to the fallow fields. Being so much farther south of Pemberley, there are even flowers still blooming in the gardens around Netherfield, though the gardener informs me that these are the last of the blooms until spring.*

*On the day of my arrival, I was forced to attend an assembly in the nearby village. As you can imagine, it was the last thing I wished to do, but Miss Bingley offered to remain home to keep me company should I not want to go. Naturally, I chose to attend the dance rather than remain alone with Miss Bingley.*

Laughter bubbled up in Georgiana as she read her brother's words. She laughed so hard at the picture his words painted and was forced to wipe the tears from her eyes before she could continue reading.

*Much to my surprise, I found that I enjoyed the experience, though I did get off to a rocky start. I avoided my dances with Mrs. Hurst and Miss Bingley and looked to find a quiet corner in which to pass the evening. Unfortunately, Bingley discovered my location and pressed me to dance, even suggesting a partner. I did not turn to look at the young woman he indicated and consequently did not realize she was within range to overhear my remarks to Bingley, which I am ashamed to admit were most unkind. However, I must admire the young lady for her apt response. Raising her voice just enough to reach my ears, she made the following comment: 'I find it surprising that some people think themselves above their company. I always thought the sign of a true gentleman was that he treated everyone he met with respect. It is sad that Mr. Bingley's friend and family do not possess his good manners.' Mortification flooded through me to realize that she was correct in her expression. I knew I should apologize and I made my way from the hot, crowded room onto the balcony to calm and gather my thoughts.*

*As I stood on the balcony, I muttered aloud, berating myself for my poor behavior. As it happened, the young lady was passing the open balcony door, and she kindly forgave me my thoughtless words. I asked her to dance and she gave me her next open set. As I waited for the set to arrive, I set myself to dancing with one of her younger sisters and her dear friend.*

*The young lady's name is Miss Elizabeth Bennet. I have since seen her on two occasions because Mr. Bingley is enamored of her elder sister. Miss Elizabeth also has three younger sisters. Her father's estate borders that of Mr. Bingley. Miss Elizabeth is a charming young lady with a sharp wit and brilliant sense of humor. She possesses a zest for life that I cannot but admire. I wish you could meet her, for I am confident you would become good friends.*

*Well, if this is to go out with the morning post, I must close for now. I pray you are improving every day. Please write*

*soon; your letters help to breach the
distance currently between us.*

*Your loving brother,
William*

Georgiana was astonished by much of her
brother's letter. He rarely made mistakes, at least
that she could see, and she could not recall ever
hearing him admit to one or apologizing. Who was
this Miss Elizabeth Bennet to have had such an
effect upon her brother? It made her wish to meet
the young lady. Georgiana had always hoped for a
close female friend or a sister; perhaps she would
someday have both.

Before returning to her practice on the
pianoforte, Georgiana sat down to respond to her
brother's letter. She asked several questions about
Miss Elizabeth Bennet. Waiting for her brother's
reply would take a great deal of patience, thought
Georgiana with a frown.

# SHOPPING IN MERYTON

WHEN TUESDAY MORNING ARRIVED, DARCY AND Bingley rode to Longbourn to meet the Bennet sisters. After brief greetings to Mrs. Bennet, the group set out down the drive for the walk into Meryton. Kitty and Lydia led the way, their heads close together in whispered conversation that frequently erupted into loud giggles. A disapproving Mary followed. She could be heard admonishing them for their behavior. Next came Bingley with Miss Bennet on his arm, followed by Darcy with Elizabeth at his side. They chatted in low tones, though the occasional flush appeared on Elizabeth's face at her younger sisters' antics.

"Please do not be concerned, Miss Elizabeth. Miss Catherine and Miss Lydia are young. With the proper guidance, they will mature, just as you and Miss Bennet did and as Miss Mary is doing."

"I appreciate your sentiments, Mr. Darcy, but my parents have not taken the time to provide that guidance. I worry that it might be too late before they take action. Lydia particularly seems to think of nothing but the soon-to-arrive militia. There are bound to be a few scoundrels among the soldiers. For all of their exuberance, my sisters have no experience with scoundrels and charmers. In our small hamlet, there are not the variety of characters to be encountered who could give them the experience necessary to recognize someone who does not have their best interests at heart."

"To ease your mind, I shall watch over them for as long as I am in the area."

"You are very kind to offer, Mr. Darcy, but they are not your responsibility."

"Nor are they yours, but you expend a great deal of concern for their wellbeing."

"I wish they would listen to Jane and me. I do not want to change them but would like to impress upon them the importance of good behavior. What would you say to them if they were your younger sisters?"

Darcy thought for several minutes as they continued walking. "If it were Georgiana, I believe I would remind her of my love for her and my desire for her happiness. After that, I might be tempted to tell her of some situations in which such unchecked behavior led the young lady into trouble."

"Please tell me any such stories of which you are aware so that I can draw on them when the opportunity presents itself."

"I shall give the matter some thought as we enjoy our outing. Perhaps I will remember something to share on our return journey."

"I thank you for your offer of assistance, Mr. Darcy."

By now the group had arrived at the village. Speeding up, Kitty and Lydia began to increase their distance from the rest of the group. They had gone only a few steps when Mr. Darcy's deep voice caused them to pause. "Miss Catherine, Miss Lydia, would you please remain with us? I am counting on your excellent taste to help me select some ribbons for my sister. Miss Mary, I hope you will assist me in finding some music for Georgiana."

"It would be my pleasure, Mr. Darcy, but what if I pick a piece that she already has?"

"Do not worry about that. We have more than one home, so Georgiana will not need to carry her music back and forth with her." Mary smiled at the attention of the distinguished Mr. Darcy.

Though Kitty and Lydia had not responded to Darcy's request, they did stop and wait for the others to catch up with them.

"Are you going to get us a ribbon, too, Mr. Darcy, for helping you?" asked the youngest Bennet sister.

"Lydia!" cried Jane and Mary, shock and embarrassment in their voices.

"Lydia! You are being rude," said a disgusted Elizabeth.

"Well, Miss Lydia, I had, indeed, considered making a gift to you for your assistance, but your sisters are correct. Asking for a gift is just not appropriate."

Bingley did not say anything but nodded his agreement.

Lydia frowned at their words. Her lips formed a pout, but she did not argue. She folded her arms across her chest and followed the others to the dry goods store to look at the ribbon selection. Kitty led the way to the back corner, where the spools of ribbons were kept.

"Tell me about Miss Darcy," said Kitty. "What is her favorite color? What color are her hair and eyes?"

"My sister is similar in coloring to Miss Bennet. I am not sure what her favorite color is, but from the amount of blue she wears, I suspect she likes that best."

Kitty moved to the spools of blue ribbon and began to look through them. Still feeling the sting of Mr. Darcy's gentle rebuke, Lydia slowly wandered, gazing at the vast assortment of ribbons. Pausing before one in particular, she looked first at the ribbon and then at her sister Jane with an expression of musing. "I think this ribbon would be lovely on Jane. Perhaps Miss Darcy would like this as well." Lydia spoke hesitantly and more quietly than was her wont, as if fearing that she might bring disapproval upon herself again. Mr. Darcy and her sisters turned to look at the ribbon that slid from the spool into the palm of her hand and through her fingers.

"That is, indeed, a beautiful color," said Darcy as he reached out his fingers to stroke the softness of the satin ribbon. "The color is hard to pin down. Some of it appears blue, but other parts seem more like green, depending upon how the light strikes it. You made an excellent choice, Miss Lydia. My thanks for your assistance." Darcy gave the girl a gentle smile—one that reached his eyes. Lydia's spirits began to lift. "Miss Kitty, perhaps you would also pick one. What is your favorite color?" he asked.

Without hesitating, Kitty said, "Rose."

"Then let us give Georgiana a choice. You should select one that you would choose for yourself."

Kitty hurried to a spool near the start of the row of ribbons. It was one she wished to purchase for herself, but she was required to wait until she received her next quarter's allowance. Kitty handed the spool to Mr. Darcy, saying, "Is it not the most lovely of colors?"

"It is, indeed," agreed Mr. Darcy. "And, I believe, the color would look lovely on you." Kitty blushed at the gentleman's compliment.

Darcy took the spools to the counter and instructed the clerk as to how much to cut. After paying for his package, Mr. Darcy said, "I believe, Miss Bennet, you mentioned something about the quality of the shawls made by one of the ladies in town. Perhaps we should go there next?"

Darcy extended his arm for the ladies to precede him from the shop. Bingley offered his arm to Jane, and the two of them led the way. The three youngest sisters followed, while Darcy brought up the rear. This time he offered his arm to Elizabeth. She placed her hand on the extended arm with a shy smile of thanks.

The party turned down one of the side streets, which was lined by several small residences. Bingley paused before the last house on the right, then opened the gate for Jane to enter. Before doing so, she looked to her sisters, remarking, "Since Mrs. Powell's house is quite small, you girls should wait here while the rest of us go inside. Please do not wander off, for we shall be on to our next stop soon."

Her sisters nodded and Mr. Bingley gallantly offered to keep them company. He bowed to Jane as she proceeded through the gate, followed by Darcy and Elizabeth.

Jane rang the bell that hung beside the door.

"One minute," came the slightly quavering female voice. The door was opened by a small woman with white hair and sparkling gray eyes. "Miss Jane, dear, how lovely to see you."

"You as well, Mrs. Powell. We have brought you a customer. Mr. Darcy wishes to purchase a shawl for his sister."

"Please come with me. I will show you the ones I currently have completed."

The elderly woman led them to a curtain on the right side of her home. When she pulled back the covering, a small room appeared. Within, the walls were covered with pegs from which hung a wide assortment of shawls of different fabrics and patterns. They each moved to a different location and began to examine the items before them. Elizabeth admired a soft, golden wool embroidered in dark green with a Greek key pattern around all of the edges. Darcy stared at those before him but felt a bit overwhelmed at making such a choice. It was Jane who found the perfect one.

"I believe Miss Darcy would find this one most useful," said Jane as she pulled a shawl from its peg and turned to show it to the others.

Darcy studied the item with his usual seriousness. However, at Elizabeth's comment of, "Oh, how lovely and practical," he decided to agree with her. The shawl Jane had found was of downy white wool embroidered with small bouquets of flowers in purple, pink, yellow, and green. Sewn across the stems of the flowers was a raised bow in a color identical to the ribbon Lydia had chosen. Darcy asked the price and stated his belief that it was worth more. Mrs. Powell refused to accept more, so Darcy took the wrapped package and, as they departed, placed three shillings on the table beside the door.

Rejoining the others, the group returned to town, to the bookstore. While Mary, Elizabeth, and

Mr. Darcy entered, Jane and Bingley followed the two youngest as they rushed from store to store, looking at the items on display.

In the bookstore, Mary looked through the music. She pulled a recently published piece from the rack. Darcy could hear her humming to herself. Her right hand seemed to move rapidly, as if it were playing the notes in front of her. With a wistful sigh, she returned it to the rack and looked through the other selections.

"What was that first piece you selected, Miss Mary?"

"It was a new piece by Beethoven."

"And do you like his music?"

"Very much, sir."

"Then if it is a new piece, perhaps my sister would enjoy it. Show me again which one it was." Mary indicated the requested music sheet. Darcy picked up two but kept them together as if one piece. "What was it you wished to suggest as a gift for my sister, Miss Elizabeth?"

Elizabeth led him to the opposite back corner of the store and stopped before a display of leather-bound journals. Before speaking, she glanced around to ensure that no one would overhear. "I thought that since Miss Darcy does not have anyone in whom to confide her feelings, she might appreciate a place where she could record them. I find that when I commit my worries and feelings to paper, it helps me let go of my concerns. Often, I discover a solution to my problems or am freed from the burdens I carry."

"That does seem to be both a beautiful and a useful suggestion." Darcy looked at the selection before him. Eventually, he selected one with a dark blue cover. He added it to the other items in his arms and moved to pay for his purchases. When they rejoined the remainder of the group, it was Bingley who suggested that they stop at the tearoom for refreshments. It was a merry group that arrived back at Longbourn upon the conclusion of the outing.

Returning to Netherfield Park laden with packages, Darcy hoped to reach his room unobserved. However, Miss Bingley rushed from the drawing room like a cat pouncing upon its prey. Darcy took a deep breath and prayed for patience as he faced the inquisitive Miss Bingley.

"Mr. Darcy, why did you and Charles not mention you were going into the village to shop? Louisa and I would have enjoyed accompanying you." Her voice changed, dripping with disdain as she continued. "Though I doubt there would be much of worth to be discovered in such a small town, particularly for a man with your discerning tastes." Changing her tone to one more coquettish, she batted her eyelashes and asked, "Who is the lucky recipient of your generosity?"

"I always purchase gifts for Georgiana when I travel. I enjoy surprising her with something from the places I visit."

"Ahh, dear Geor—Miss Darcy. How I long to see her again. Indeed, Mr. Darcy, Louisa and I would have enjoyed helping you make selections for your delightful sister, would we not, Louisa?"

Mrs. Hurst nodded enthusiastically. "I do hope you were able to choose things that Miss Darcy will enjoy. We would have been of much more assistance than Charles. Ladies are much better at knowing what another lady would like."

"True," Miss Bingley agreed.

"I believe I am well acquainted with my sister's preferences." Darcy's tone was cold. "Besides, I was looking for something unique to the area. As you only recently took up residence in the area, I doubt you are aware of the notable craftsmen in the vicinity."

Contempt coloring her tone, Miss Bingley added, "I doubt Meryton offers any items special enough for a young lady of Miss Darcy's exquisite taste." She and Mrs. Hurst tittered. The genuine, melodious laughter of Miss Elizabeth Bennet flitted through Darcy's mind and compared favorably to the affected way in which these ladies laughed.

Noticing that his friend's patience was wearing thin, Bingley spoke up. "Mr. Darcy did not need to rely on my opinions. We escorted the Misses Bennet to Meryton. They showed us the best shops and helped choose gifts for Miss Darcy."

As he watched the expressions of the two ladies darken, Darcy wished he could have escaped from the drawing room before mention was made of the Bennet sisters. It was a topic that always brought out the worst in Bingley's siblings. "Really, Charles, how could you let such unsophisticated and inelegant ladies help select gifts for Miss Darcy?" Caroline asked. "She will certainly be disappointed by the selections and it will reflect poorly on our family."

Not wishing to listen to the disparagement of the young ladies that was sure to follow, Darcy said, "Please excuse me. I should like to wrap these into one package to send to Georgiana." With a curt nod, Darcy departed.

He had not reached the stairs when he heard Miss Bingley's sharp voice: "Charles, you must stop forcing Mr. Darcy into such disgraceful company or he may decide to return to town. A gentleman of his status will not wish to associate with such country misses–particularly the youngest three, who are either utterly boring or totally out of control." Darcy shook his head. Miss Bingley's strident voice faded into nothingness as he climbed the stairs.

Once he reached his suite, Darcy rang for his valet, Evans, whom he asked to place the items in the closet. He would hold them until he received Georgiana's next letter, then send some–or all–of them along to her with his next message. Taking a seat before the fire in his room, he accepted the small glass of brandy and sipped it as he thought about the morning's outing. As he reflected on his interactions with the three youngest Bennet sisters, a thought struck him. Each of them had responded to his attention and kind words. He recalled Elizabeth once saying that her father referred to them as the silliest girls in England. Was their more outlandish behavior the result of their father's lack of attention? Darcy would discuss the possibility with Miss Elizabeth when next they met. Perhaps the same was true with Mrs. Bennet. From his observations of the interactions between Mr. and Mrs. Bennet, the gentleman openly mocked his wife and purposely caused her distress. Could the same steady attempt to guide both mother and younger daughters help to ease Miss Elizabeth's worry and frequent embarrassment? Darcy gave the situation more thought and planned to discuss it with Bingley.

From there, his thoughts wandered to Georgiana. She would receive his letter today or tomorrow, and he wondered what her reaction would be. Darcy sincerely hoped that his dear sister was regaining her former good spirits. Georgiana had always been shy, but she was a happy girl with a warm heart. He would gladly pummel Wickham to death for the hurt Georgiana had received at the scoundrel's hands.

After enjoying his drink and some quiet contemplation, Darcy quietly made his way to Bingley's study to deal with a packet of correspondence from his steward at Pemberley. Evans had informed him that the package had arrived during his outing. Darcy dealt with every item before returning to his room to change for dinner.

As he descended the stairs to the drawing room, Caroline Bingley's complaining reached his ears. "Whatever can we do, Louisa, to discourage Charles and Mr. Darcy from spending so much time with Miss Bennet and Miss Eliza? You do not think Mr. Darcy could truly be attracted to her, do you? Why can the gentleman not see that I am his perfect match? Our interests are similar, we both have excellent style, and he finds my humor amusing, as evidenced by his pithy remarks. I am elegant, well-educated, and experienced with the ton and with entertaining."

Darcy was aghast at hearing himself described as similar to Miss Bingley. However, as he recalled his thoughtless words at the assembly, it was not surprising if she considered him so. Darcy determined immediately that he would work at being more outgoing and friendly. Perhaps if he observed Miss Elizabeth, he might discover the secret to her not-inconsiderable social skill. Straightening his waistcoat, Darcy stood taller and prepared to enter the room. He paused as Miss Bingley spoke again.

"How can I draw his attention from that country miss to myself, where it belongs? I had counted on Mr. Darcy proposing while we were alone here in the country." Caroline stamped her foot in frustration. "There must be something I can do. If his distraction grows, perhaps it may be necessary to compromise him and take away his options. I cannot lose the gentleman to such a nobody as Miss Eliza. Nor can we allow Charles to waste himself on Miss Bennet. She might make for pleasant company while we are forced to remain in this wilderness, but she brings neither fortune nor connections to a marriage that can advance our family in society."

Knowing he would have to be on his guard to protect both himself and Miss Elizabeth, Darcy stepped more forcefully upon the stairs to alert the ladies as to his presence. If Hurst fell asleep as the gentlemen lingered over drinks after dinner, Darcy would inform Bingley of what he overheard. Pasting on a smile, Darcy entered the drawing room.

"Good evening, Miss Bingley, Mrs. Hurst." Darcy's tone was stiff and formal. He crossed the room and poured himself a drink before taking up his usual stance at the window. Fortunately, Charles and Hurst entered soon after Darcy, sparing him from having to make small talk with Bingley's sisters. He did wish to improve his demeanor in company, but any familiarity he showed to Caroline Bingley would only convince her that she would achieve her desires. Darcy thought to himself, *I would not marry Caroline if she were the last woman in the world.*

# MUCH TO CONSIDER

ENSCONCED IN THE LIBRARY, DARCY HAD rested his book on his lap as his thoughts returned to the events of the previous evening. A dinner party at the Gouldings' gave Darcy the opportunity for which he was looking. Upon arriving, he noticed Miss Elizabeth in conversation with her elder sister and dear friend, Miss Charlotte Lucas. After greeting his hosts, Darcy and Bingley made their way across the room to join the group of ladies.

"Good evening, Miss Lucas, Miss Bennet, Miss Elizabeth," said Darcy as he bowed to them. Bingley echoed his friend's welcome as the group exchanged greetings. "I hope we are not interrupting anything by joining you."

"Not at all, Mr. Darcy. I was just sharing with Jane and Lizzy the news that Meryton will play host to a militia unit for the winter." Miss Lucas had barely finished speaking before loud squeals came from the corner where Lydia, Kitty, and Maria Lucas stood. Their faces flushed with embarrassment, Jane and Elizabeth looked at each other and shook their heads.

Unfortunately, their disgrace was not over, as Mrs. Bennet's loud voice reached all corners of the room. "A militia unit! Oh, how wonderful. I once loved a man in a red coat. With the addition of so many gentlemen to the neighborhood, I shall surely find husbands for all of my girls."

Their blushes deepening, Miss Bennet and Miss Elizabeth looked at the floor, both wishing it would open up and swallow them.

"Miss Bennet, Miss Elizabeth, please do not be embarrassed. This type of reaction is not unusual for such news. When in the company of my cousin, Colonel Fitzwilliam, I have often observed that the ladies seem drawn to a man in uniform. There are an unscrupulous few who know that the uniform causes such an effect, and they wear it to take advantage of unsuspecting young ladies. I will caution your father to beware while the militia is in residence in Meryton."

Elizabeth's relieved smile warmed Darcy. "Your understanding is greatly appreciated, Mr. Darcy. My sisters are at a difficult and confusing age. They are more aware of their abilities and the world around them. They wish to enchant young men, but their youth and inexperience could cause situations to arise which they are ill-equipped to handle."

Wishing to spare the ladies further discomfort, Darcy asked them about their recent activities. The conversation continued naturally, with the group moving from topic to topic. As others joined or departed the group, Darcy made a point of speaking to them and continuing to engage in conversation, no matter how mundane or nonsensical the topic.

As Darcy pondered the matter, he realized that his comfort in Miss Elizabeth's presence contributed significantly to his ability to relax and join in the conversation of those around him. Darcy wondered what it would be like to always be so comfortable in company. Would having

Elizabeth in his life provide him with the comfort that was so often missing?

His review of the evening, and the upcoming arrival of the militia unit, made Darcy wonder what he could say to Mr. Bennet that would not be considered interference in his family's affairs. Then inspiration struck. Darcy would contact his cousin, Richard, to discover if he had any leave. If Richard joined Darcy at Netherfield Park, it would provide him with an additional layer of protection from Miss Bingley. Richard might also be able to attract sufficient interest from the youngest Misses Bennet to keep the riffraff in the militia away from the young ladies. Darcy moved across the room to the writing desk, where he pulled out a sheet of paper, sharpened a quill, and began writing. He had finished the letter and was about to reach for the bell pull when a knock came at the door. Darcy called, "Come," and the butler entered.

"You must be a mind-reader, Dawson. Could you please see that this letter is sent by express immediately?"

"Certainly, sir." Dawson extended a salver, on which Darcy placed the letter. Before Darcy turned away, the butler said, "This letter just arrived for you, sir."

"Thank you, Dawson." Darcy took the letter from the tray as the butler bowed and exited the library. Returning to his chair, Darcy studied the envelope. He noted his sister's familiar hand. With a smile, he broke the seal and began to read.

*Pemberley*
*Derbyshire*
*25 October 1811*

*Dear William,*

*I was delighted to receive your most recent letter. Mr. Bingley's estate and the surrounding neighborhood sound lovely. I wish it were possible to join you there and see it for myself.*

*I was also interested to learn about your new acquaintances. I believe it is the first time you have ever written to me about a young lady. Miss Elizabeth Bennet sounds delightful and just the sort of person I wish I had for a friend. Do you think she would like me? Do you think she might be willing to correspond with me?*

*Some of your comments even made me laugh out loud. Life has offered little reason for laughter over the last few months, and I forgot how much lighter I feel when I laugh. I like the feeling and will look for the whimsical in my daily life.*

*With only your letter by which to judge, I believe you are enjoying your trip more than usual. I hope to hear more of your new friends and adventures in Hertfordshire in your next letter. Please write soon.*

*Love,*
*Georgie*

Darcy felt his heart lighten to learn that his words had caused such a reaction in his dear sister. *Though I could not experience her laughter first-hand, I am delighted to have inspired it in her,* Darcy thought with a satisfied smile. He pulled a sheet of paper out of his writing desk and began his letter.

> *Netherfield Park*
> *Hertfordshire*
> *October 30, 1811*
>
> *Dearest Georgie,*
>
> *How delighted I am to learn that my letter brought you laughter. I only wish I could have heard the delightful sound for myself. I am enclosing several packages with this letter. I numbered them, so please open them in order. I shall tell you about each of the Bennet sisters, as they helped me select these for you.*
>
> *Open package one. The two youngest Bennet sisters, Miss Kitty and Miss Lydia, chose these items for you. These two sisters are an interesting study. The elder, Miss Catherine (called Kitty by her family), follows her younger sister, Miss Lydia, in all her adventures. They are a bit excitable, but not truly bad girls. Miss Lydia, who is the youngest, is also a bit spoiled, but she behaved prettily with only minor correction. I feel a little sorry for the girls, as they are often called 'the silliest girls in England' by their eccentric father. Before making their selections, they asked about your appearance and favorite color. Miss Lydia was thoughtful in her choice, selecting the blue/green ribbon. I asked*

*Miss Kitty to pick out one in her favorite color, and the rose was her choice.*

*Unwrap the package marked number two. Miss Mary Bennet chose the sheet music for you. She is the middle daughter and dedicated to improving herself. To her disadvantage, Miss Mary's choice of sermons as reading material makes for less-than-stimulating conversation. She also loves to play the pianoforte but never received the benefit of a master. Miss Mary's technique is excellent, but it lacks the emotion that makes your music so enjoyable. I believe she could use a friend. Being in the middle, she is not part of the tight friendships of either her older or younger sisters.*

*Open gift three. This selection was the choice of Miss Jane Bennet, the eldest sister. She asked much about your clothing preferences and chose this because it would complement much of your wardrobe. A widow in the nearby village of Meryton made the shawl. Meryton is much like Lambton, though somewhat smaller.*

*Now you may open the last parcel. In my previous letter, I spoke to you much about Miss Elizabeth. With her vast experience with sisters, I put your situation to her without naming you. Please do not be anxious; Miss Elizabeth was quite angry with the gentleman in my story. She quickly recognized that he was the villain in taking advantage of someone so much younger. In fact, she worries for her youngest sisters, as a militia unit will soon be wintering in Meryton. Miss Elizabeth advised that in a situation in which a young woman lacks a close confidante with whom to share her experiences, a journal can serve as that friend. It gives you a safe place for expressing yourself without worry that anyone will judge you for your feelings.*

*It is my sincere hope that you are improving every day. I love you, dear sister, and wish you the best. I will be home in time to join you for Christmas.*

*Love,*
*William*

# A SHORT STAY AT NETHERFIELD

Caroline Bingley grew more frustrated with each passing day. No matter how often she impressed upon her brother and Mr. Darcy about the poor behavior of Mrs. Bennet and her three youngest daughters, nothing seemed to deter the gentleman from their interest in the eldest two Bennet sisters. Realizing that she needed more information with which to discredit the family, Caroline invited Miss Jane Bennet to tea. Unfortunately for Jane, Mrs. Bennet insisted that she ride to Netherfield when it threatened to rain. Jane arrived soaked and felt increasingly unwell.

As a consequence, Jane answered Miss Bingley's rather impertinent questions with her usual honesty. She did not recognize Miss Bingley's insulting demeanor and haughty tone. Just as the ladies were hinting to their guest that the time of departure was upon them, Jane fainted. With a seriously displeased tone, Miss Bingley called for the housekeeper and a footman to take Miss Bennet to one of the guest rooms.

Learning what was wanted, the housekeeper called for a maid and rushed to prepare a bedchamber. The footman had just begun to mount the stairs when the gentlemen returned home from a dinner with the officers from the soon-to-arrive militia. The gentlemen had left early because of the steadily increasing rain.

"What is the matter with Miss Bennet?" Bingley cried as he noticed the footman holding, in his arms, the woman whom Bingley was rapidly coming to love. He rushed forward and said to the footman, "James, allow me to carry her."

"Charles, desist immediately. If this woman were to awaken, she could claim a compromise."

"Now is not the time, Caroline. I will take Miss Bennet to the blue guestroom. You should call for Mr. Jones, the apothecary, to come and check on her." Turning away, Bingley mounted the stairs and turned to the right, towards the guest wing. When he reached the blue room, the fire was burning brightly in the grate and the bed was turned down. Upon depositing Miss Bennet on the bed, Bingley wished to linger, but the housekeeper requested that he remove himself so they could attend to the young lady.

Caroline watched her brother's retreating back as she muttered under her breath about "this wretched place." At least that was what it sounded like to Darcy. Once Miss Bingley had moved to the writing desk in the drawing room to compose a note to the apothecary, Darcy turned to the butler, Dawson. "Would you ask my coachman, Mr. Henry, to join me in Mr. Bingley's study?"

"Certainly, sir."

Darcy continued down the hall to Bingley's study. He seated himself behind the desk. At a knock on the door, he called, "Come."

Dawson appeared in the doorway. "Mr. Henry to see you, sir."

"Thank you, Dawson."

As the butler bowed out and closed the door, the coachman spoke. "You wished to see me, Mr. Darcy."

"Yes, I need your expert opinion on the state of the roads. Would it be possible for my coach to make it to Longbourn and back in the next hour or two, or will the roads be impassable?"

The man thought for a moment, then said, "What exactly is it you need me to do, sir?"

"Miss Bennet took ill while having tea with the ladies earlier today. I am sure she would be greatly comforted if her sister, Miss Elizabeth, stayed with and cared for her during her illness. I want to send you with a note and have you wait while Miss Elizabeth packs for herself and her sister. Then you will return to Netherfield with Miss Elizabeth and their trunks."

Mr. Henry nodded. "If would be better if a footman went ahead of me to alert the young lady and allow her to do the packing, as we should make the return journey without delay, sir. The rain is tapering off, but we cannot be sure that it will not pick up again."

"That is an excellent suggestion. If you wait, I will write the note. You can ask one of our men to take it."

"Yes, sir."

As Darcy pulled the writing supplies from the desk, the coachman stood nearby, nervously turning his cap in his hand.

*Netherfield Park*
*Meryton*
*3 November 1811*

*Dear Miss Elizabeth,*

*Please pardon me for writing you directly, but I thought you would wish to know that Miss Bennet took ill after tea and fainted. The apothecary should arrive shortly to examine her.*

*I believe that Miss Bennet would prefer your care to that of either Miss Bingley or Mrs. Hurst. Consequently, my coach and driver will arrive within the next hour to bring you to Netherfield Park. I hope that will allow you sufficient time to pack belongings for the both of you.*

*Please try not to worry. By the time you arrive, we should know your sister's condition.*

*Sincerely,*
*Fitzwilliam Darcy*

After sanding and sealing the note, Darcy handed it to Mr. Henry. "The message informs Miss Elizabeth that you will arrive in an hour. She should be ready to leave upon your arrival. Please drive carefully, Mr. Henry, to ensure that you both return here safely."

"Of course, Mr. Darcy. I shall take good care of the young lady."

When he completed his business, Mr. Darcy moved to rejoin his hosts in the parlor. As he approached the door, he became aware of Miss Bingley's raised voice.

"Charles, what were you thinking to carry Miss Bennet like that? She is just the type of scheming woman to claim a compromise."

"Do not be ridiculous, Caroline. Miss Bennet is not the type of woman to act in such a manner. Besides, I rather think I would very much like being married to Miss Bennet. She is the loveliest and kindest woman I have ever met.

Miss Bingley paled at her brother's words. "Charles, I forbid you to waste yourself on a young woman of no fortune and consequence. For instance, I learned today over tea that the Bennets' uncle is in trade and lives in Cheapside. We have worked so hard to rise above our roots in trade. If you married Miss Bennet, you would be dragging us down, not helping to raise us in society, as father wished. I will not allow you to ruin my chances of marrying well by making such a mistake. I demand that you stop this ridiculous infatuation immediately." Caroline stamped her foot for emphasis.

Darcy cleared his throat and approached the entry. Though he directed his gaze at Bingley, he could not fail to observe the anger and irritation on his hostess's face. "Bingley, I hope you will not mind, but I sent my carriage and a note to bring Miss Elizabeth here. I am sure Miss Bennet will be more comfortable with her sister to care for her. I also knew that Miss Elizabeth would worry a great deal when Miss Bennet did not return home tonight."

"That is an excellent idea, Darcy. Thank you for thinking of it. I will let Mrs. Dawson know to prepare another guest room." Bingley made his way from the room while Darcy sat and took up his book. The swish, swish, swish of Miss Bingley's skirts as she paced was the only sound in the room.

Finally, she came to a halt in front of his chair. "Mr. Darcy, you must help me to convince Charles to end this childish infatuation and return to town. He could make a much better match with any of the young ladies he would meet in London."

"I am sorry to disappoint you, Miss Bingley, but I will not interfere with your brother's personal affairs. I am happy to help him learn to manage an estate, but that is as far as my influence will extend."

"How can you not realize the risk that such a young woman poses to my brother? Are you not his dearest friend? Why would you not wish to save him from himself?"

"Miss Bingley, your brother is an adult. He is better able to judge the state of his heart than either you or I. Charles knows best what will make him happy."

Caroline realized she would not change his mind at present, but refused to concede the issue. "Since you have invited Miss Eliza Bennet to join her sister here, I must caution you, Mr. Darcy, to take care of yourself. There is not a doubt in my mind that this chit is a scheming fortune hunter."

"Miss Bingley, I must ask you to keep your opinions to yourself. Both Miss Bennet and Miss Elizabeth are gentlewomen and their behavior is always above reproach. Miss Elizabeth has become a good friend during our stay here in Hertfordshire. I do not wish to hear your reproaches of her again."

Caroline ground her teeth in frustration and rushed from the room. Darcy breathed a sigh of relief at her departure.

Miss Lizzy, there is a message for you," said Mrs. Hill as she entered the parlor.

Elizabeth looked up, surprise in her expression, as she reached to take the message from the housekeeper. She looked at the handwriting but did not recognize it other than to note its decided masculinity. Elizabeth broke the seal and read the note before tucking it into her pocket.

"Who was it from, Lizzy? What does it say?"

"Jane is so unwell, she fainted. They sent for Mr. Jones. I am invited to stay and care for Jane until she recovers. I need to hurry and pack, for a coach will be here shortly to take me to Netherfield."

After calling for their maid, Susie, to begin the packing, Elizabeth knocked on the door of her father's study.

"Come."

"Papa," said Elizabeth as she entered the room. "Jane got soaked on her ride to Netherfield and became ill enough to faint. I am invited to come and stay for the duration of her illness. I will be leaving in just over half an hour. Is there a message you wish me to give to Jane?"

The stern look his second daughter gave him caused Mr. Bennet to feel regret for not having insisted that Jane take the carriage. "Please tell Jane that I hope she recovers quickly. I also understand your hidden message. I should have been firmer with your mother. I will speak with her after you leave, and I promise to speak up should she try such a stunt again in the future. Be well, my Lizzy, and come home soon. With both you and Jane absent, there will not be a word of sense spoken while you are gone."

"Perhaps you should spend some time with Mary and suggest something new for her to read, as well as require her to discuss it with you. I believe all of your daughters have the potential to be like Jane and me, but they need your attention just as we had."

Elizabeth kissed her father's cheek and rushed upstairs to finish the packing so that she would not keep Mr. Darcy's coachman waiting. By the time the carriage arrived in front of Longbourn, Elizabeth was waiting in the hallway with two small trunks containing clothes for Jane and herself.

As she tied the ribbons on her bonnet, Elizabeth paused in the parlor door to say, "Goodbye, Mama, Mary, Kitty, Lydia."

"Do not hurry back," Mrs. Bennet called after her. "You must allow time for Mr. Bingley to propose to Jane. I do not want you back until Jane is engaged."

Elizabeth did not answer; she just rolled her eyes at Mrs. Hill as the housekeeper helped with her cloak.

Two footmen knocked on the front door. The first one assisted Elizabeth into the carriage, then returned to help load the trunks. When everything was in place, they jumped on the back and the carriage took off down the drive.

Elizabeth took a moment to wonder why it was Mr. Darcy who had sent the message to her. Such a responsibility usually fell to the hostess of a home. Elizabeth chuckled to realize how unlikely it was that Miss Bingley would issue her an invitation to stay at Netherfield. With that in mind, Elizabeth recognized the kindness of Mr. Darcy. He must be coming to know her well to realize how much Elizabeth would desire to care for her sister.

When she arrived at Netherfield, Mr. Darcy was waiting to receive her. "Miss Elizabeth, I hope you had enough time before the carriage arrived."

"Yes, Mr. Darcy. Your plans were perfect. I am grateful for your consideration and invitation. I hope Mr. Bingley does not mind my arrival.

"I am happy to answer your question, but as Mr. Jones is still with Miss Bennet, you may wish to go up and join them."

"Thank you, Mr. Darcy. I would indeed like to join them."

"Allow me to show you the way."

Darcy led Elizabeth up the stairs and into the guest wing. He paused before the door of Miss Bennet's chamber. "I will wait here in case you need anything," offered Darcy.

"That is most kind of you, sir, but I doubt that will be necessary. I am sure there is a servant to fetch anything that may be needed."

"If you are sure, I shall wait downstairs. However, please do not hesitate to call on me if you should need anything."

"Thank you for your kind offer. I will avail myself of it should it become necessary." Elizabeth gave him a warm smile before slipping into Jane's room.

Darcy joined his friend in the study as they waited for the apothecary's report.

"Do you think she will be well?" Bingley asked, worry in his voice.

Darcy took the chair next to his before the fire. He reached for the decanter on the table between the chairs, then held it out to his friend. At Bingley's nod, Darcy topped off his glass before pouring himself a small portion of brandy.

"She most likely took a chill from getting wet. I am sure that with some rest and nourishment, she will be well. You can be confident that Miss Elizabeth will take good care of her dearest sister."

"Of course, you are correct. We must be sure that Miss Elizabeth has whatever she needs to care for Miss Bennet."

Darcy nodded his head in agreement. "I already informed Miss Elizabeth to let me know of anything she may need."

The gentlemen sipped quietly, each lost in his thoughts. They were interrupted by a knock at the door. "Mr. Jones to see you, sir."

The gentlemen rose and greeted the apothecary. "How is Miss Bennet, sir?" asked an anxious Bingley.

"Miss Bennet suffers from a severe cold. I left some powders to help her sleep. I am sure that with rest and nourishment, she will make a complete recovery. While running a fever, she should take only broth and tea. However, when her fever breaks. She can eat whatever she wishes."

"She is welcome to stay for as long as needed. Please do not rush her recovery, Mr. Jones, for I would not wish her to suffer a relapse."

"That is kind of you, Mr. Bingley. Miss Bennet will need to remain in bed for several days—even after the fever ends."

"She will have everything she needs, sir."

"I will return tomorrow to check on my patient. Goodnight, gentlemen." Bingley rang for a servant and Dawson arrived to lead the apothecary to the door.

"I believe I will ask Caroline to check on Miss Bennet and ensure that Miss Elizabeth has everything she needs to provide for her sister's care." Darcy looked dubious at his friend's words but did not share his thoughts.

After dressing for dinner, Darcy presented himself at Miss Bennet's door. A relieved Elizabeth answered his knock. "Is everything well, Miss Elizabeth?"

Elizabeth hesitated to answer. She knew that being truthful would cause more hard feelings from Miss Bingley. However, Elizabeth was in need of assistance. "Mrs. Dawson was kind enough to send up cool water and rags to allow me to cool Jane's brow. Unfortunately, the water is no longer cool, and there is no maid to assist in bringing more."

Darcy was not surprised by Elizabeth's words, nor did he intend to allow Miss Bingley's poor manners to go undisclosed. "I will ensure that one of my footmen is stationed in the hall to assist you should you need help. Would you like me to have a maid sit with Miss Bennet so that you might join us for dinner? You cannot neglect your health if you intend to care for your sister."

"I will not do so, Mr. Darcy, but I believe it would be best for me to request a tray so that I can stay with Jane and continue to try to bring down her fever."

"Upon arriving downstairs, I will happily speak to Mrs. Dawson for you. I will ensure that more cold water and dinner are sent up to you."

"Thank you for your assistance, Mr. Darcy. Enjoy your evening."

"Should the opportunity present itself, please join us downstairs whenever possible."

"Thank you, again. You are very considerate of our needs."

"Have a pleasant evening, Miss Elizabeth. I hope Miss Bennet will show improvement soon."

Darcy bowed and moved off down the hallway. Elizabeth smiled her thanks and remained holding the door until he disappeared from sight.

Trying to overcome the poor impression she had made earlier in the day, Miss Bingley made a fuss over him when Darcy entered the drawing room. He gave her the briefest of nods before moving to look out of the window. When the butler announced dinner, Darcy waited until the others left the room before speaking privately with Dawson. "Would you please ask Mrs. Dawson to send up cold water and dinner to Miss Bennet's room?"

"Very well, sir."

Darcy hurried to take his place at the table. The only remaining seat was beside Miss Bingley, forcing Darcy to listen to her endless compliments and complaints. When the meal finally ended, Darcy, Bingley, and Hurst lingered over their drinks. Hurst guzzled down his port and then poured another glass. After downing that as well, he leaned back in his chair. Soon, a soft snore emanated from his seat at the table.

"Do you think Miss Bennet is improved?"

"I fear not. I stopped by to see Miss Elizabeth on my way to dinner. She informed me that she was still battling to bring down Miss Bennet's fever. Surprisingly, she did not have anyone to fetch her more cold water. I informed her that I would station a footman there to assist her, but I cannot imagine why no maid was assigned to help her."

Bingley looked confused. "I did ask Caroline to check on her and to ensure that everything was as it should be."

"Perhaps you should double check and be more specific."

Bingley rang the bell and summoned the housekeeper. "Mrs. Dawson, did Miss Bingley give you any instructions regarding our guests and Miss Bennet's care?"

The housekeeper would not meet his eyes. "Miss Bingley gave no instructions, sir. I asked if a maid should be assigned to assist Miss Elizabeth, but Miss Bingley did not feel it was necessary. I felt the need for a maid to run errands, but did not wish to do so without the mistress's permission, sir."

Feeling troubled, Bingley said, "Perhaps, we should join the ladies."

Darcy nodded. Bingley shook his brother-in-law and announced that they were adjourning to the drawing room.

As the gentlemen crossed the hall, Miss Bingley's whiney voice reached them. "It is bad enough that Miss Bennet took ill while at Netherfield, but now we are saddled with the impertinent Miss Eliza as well. We must convince Mr. Jones that Miss Bennet would recover much better at home than here." Bingley frowned as he listened to his sister's comments while Darcy's irritation with his hostess grew.

Miss Bingley had barely finished speaking when the gentlemen entered the room. From the look of irritation on Charles' face, she feared he might have overheard her comments.

Darcy seated himself in the chair next to the sofa that Charles chose. Sitting directly across from his sister, Charles stared at Caroline while asking, "What did you discover when you asked after Miss Bennet?"

"I do not understand your question, Charles."

"I asked you to check with Miss Elizabeth and see what she needed to care for her sister. What did you discover?"

"I did not speak with Miss Eliza but did ask Mrs. Dawson to ensure things were as they should be."

"What specific information did you give to the housekeeper?" Bingley prodded.

Miss Bingley stuttered a moment before settling on the perfect reply. "I know nothing about caring for the ill, so I did not give any instructions. Mrs. Dawson cares for the ill staff and tenants. She should know, better than I, what needs to be done."

"If your education did not include caring for the ill or tenants, then it lacked something significant. The mistress of any estate—particularly a very large one—is responsible for the care of her staff and tenants," murmured Darcy. "I would not consider anyone for a wife who could not handle those duties."

Miss Bingley's face flushed in embarrassment.

"Did you at least assign a maid to assist Miss Elizabeth?" Charles asked.

"Charles, you are aware that we are still short-staffed; no one can be spared to help the Bennet sisters. I am sure they are used to doing for themselves, as I know they employ only a few servants."

"Bingley, I would suggest that you talk to the leasing agent. I am sure he could recommend someone who might be able to assist Miss Bennet and Miss Elizabeth. Alternatively, perhaps Miss Elizabeth is aware of someone who would be suited and needs the work."

"That is an excellent idea, Darcy. Perhaps we should check on Miss Bennet and speak to Miss Elizabeth."

"You need not bother, Charles. I will take care of this."

"Caroline, you admitted that you know nothing about this area. Therefore, I believe it would be best for me to attend to finding the necessary help to ensure that Miss Bennet has what she needs to recover."

With that, Darcy and Bingley rose and exited the drawing room. As they mounted the steps, they heard the crash of breaking china—the usual sign of Miss Bingley's uncontrolled temper.

Leaving the cloth on Jane's forehead, Elizabeth responded to the knock at the door. She was startled to see Mr. Bingley and Mr. Darcy. "Good evening, gentlemen."

"Miss Elizabeth, how is Miss Bennet this evening?" The almost pleading look on Bingley's face caused Elizabeth to smile. She was glad to report that her sister's fever was lower, but not gone. "That is excellent news. My sister informed me that we are short-staffed and that is why a maid was not assigned to assist you. Mr. Darcy suggested that perhaps you know of someone in the neighborhood who might like the position of helping with Miss Bennet's care. If she performs well, there may be a more permanent position for her."

Elizabeth thought for a moment. "I believe young Sally Foster is of an age for employment as a maid. Her parents are tenants at Longbourn. She is a bit shy but is a pleasant girl with a sweet demeanor. Sally would be an asset to any home."

"If you would write a note to her, Miss Elizabeth, we can deliver it early tomorrow morning. Perhaps Miss Foster could start the same day."

"Once Jane is asleep, I will write the note and ask your footman to deliver it to you, Mr. Darcy. Mrs. Dawson knows where the Fosters live. Thank you, gentlemen, for your care and concern. I greatly appreciate your inviting me to stay and care for Jane."

"I am sorry that your sister is ill, but we are delighted to have you both with us," said Bingley with a bright smile. "I hope your sister will be much improved by the morning. We will check on you again then. Good night, Miss Elizabeth."

Darcy lingered as Bingley headed for his chambers. "Are you well, Miss Elizabeth? Will you be able to get some rest tonight when your sister does?"

Elizabeth gave Darcy a warm smile. "I am well, sir, and I promise to rest as much as possible. Perhaps if Sally comes, I will be able to take a brief walk tomorrow and get a quick nap if necessary."

"Please, no matter the time, send Chase to me if you should need anything during the night."

Elizabeth blushed at the care he showed her. "I do not have the words to thank you for your thoughtfulness. Good night, Mr. Darcy."

"Sweet dreams, Miss Elizabeth."

At his words, the blush on her face deepened.

# CARE FOR THE CAREGIVER

EARLY THE NEXT MORNING, ELIZABETH APPEARED in the dining room. Thankfully, the only person present was Mr. Darcy. He stood at her entrance. "Good morning, Miss Elizabeth. How is Miss Bennet this morning?" Though he was concerned for her sister's illness, Darcy was more concerned for Elizabeth, as dark shadows ringed her lovely eyes.

"Jane's fever broke a little over an hour ago. She is sleeping peacefully at the moment."

Darcy moved to hold a chair for her beside his place. "You must have had a difficult night. Please allow me to fix you a plate."

"You need not wait on me, sir. I—"

Interrupting her, Darcy said, "You cared for your sister throughout the night. Please allow me to take care of you for a moment."

Too tired to argue, Elizabeth merely said, "Thank you, Mr. Darcy."

"What may I get you?"

Elizabeth pondered the selection on the sideboard. "A small portion of eggs, a slice of ham, a muffin, and tea, please."

Darcy fixed her plate and set it before her on the table before returning to prepare a cup of tea. He set down her cup and resumed his seat. "I am pleased that your sister is improving. The note to Miss Foster was delivered at seven this morning. If we receive her reply soon, I would like to accompany you on a brief walk, allowing you to get some fresh air. Then you should rest while Miss Foster tends to your sister."

"I believe fresh air would do wonders for me. I would enjoy that. Thank you for your thoughtfulness, Mr. Darcy."

The two of them enjoyed a pleasant conversation as they broke their fast. It was briefly interrupted by Mrs. Dawson, who announced the arrival of Sally Foster. Before Elizabeth could develop a response, Darcy said, "Mrs. Dawson, will you please review Miss Bennet's care needs with Sally? I am going to escort Miss Elizabeth on a walk and then insist that she rest. Can you and the new maid handle things for a few hours?"

"Certainly, sir. I believe your suggestions for Miss Elizabeth are just what she needs. We will take good care of Miss Bennet. Don't you worry, miss."

Typically, having someone speak for her would annoy Elizabeth, but instead she experienced a warm feeling in the pit of her stomach. At Longbourn, no one except Jane worried over her.

"Oh, Mrs. Dawson. Would you please ask someone to bring down Miss Elizabeth's pelisse and bonnet so that we may take our walk when we are finished eating?"

"Yes, sir, right away."

William and Elizabeth were fortunate enough to finish their meal before any of the others arrived in the dining room. They departed through the terrace doors, where Darcy offered his arm to his companion. The morning air was crisp and the dew on the grass sparkled in the sun of a bright new day. They wandered through the formal gardens in silence. When they reached the end of the pathway, they stepped into the meadow. The trees on the border of the field retained some of their leaves, but those that had fallen crunched underfoot. They continued their ramble until they reached the large pond on the garden's eastern edge.

"Would you care to sit for a moment?" asked Darcy as he gestured to the fallen tree, out of which a bench had been carved.

Elizabeth nodded and took a seat. She tipped her head back and turned her face to the sun. Despite the cold air, she enjoyed the warmth of the golden sun, which heated her cheeks. A soft sigh escaped Elizabeth, causing Darcy to chuckle. Without looking at him, Elizabeth asked, "What causes your laughter, Mr. Darcy?"

"Just a random thought. I would not wish to offend you."

"I believe we are well-enough acquainted with each other that I will not take offense."

"Your enjoyment of the outdoors brought to mind a wood nymph. Your size and coloring and the way you basked in the sun made the comparison to those mythical creatures very natural."

Elizabeth never changed positions, but a broad smile appeared on her face. "I am not offended, Mr. Darcy. Rather, I will thank you for the compliment, as nymphs were considered to be quite beautiful."

"That is, indeed, why the comparison is very apt," he agreed. Darcy noted with pleasure the blush that suffused her face. His smile grew.

They sat in silence as Darcy enjoyed the beauty before him. Elizabeth attempted to hide a yawn, but Darcy noticed it. He stood and offered his hand to his companion. "Let us return to the house. You need to rest so that you will be refreshed to return to your sister."

Elizabeth planned to ask for a few more minutes, but another yawn prevented her from speaking. She opened her eyes to see Mr. Darcy standing before her with his hand outstretched. Smiling up at him, she placed her hand in his and allowed him to pull her to her feet. Darcy then wrapped her arm around his elbow and tucked it close to his side. Together, they strolled back to the house. The hall was empty except for a footman. Darcy escorted Elizabeth up to her room. He bowed over her hand and wished her a pleasant sleep.

After leaving Elizabeth, Darcy went to Bingley's library and settled himself at the table in the corner. He was not visible from the door, but should Miss Bingley enter, there was a door to the balcony that he could use. From there, steps led to the gardens. When residing with Miss Bingley, be it at Pemberley or there at Netherfield, Darcy made it a point to never enter a room that had only one exit. He did not doubt that Miss Bingley would attempt a compromise should the opportunity present itself.

Darcy was able to work for several hours without interruption. He heard Miss Bingley enter the room and assumed that she gazed about. When she did not see him, he heard her sigh of frustration and the firm tap-tap-tap of her heels as she walked away.

Elizabeth slept through lunch before refreshing herself and returning to Jane. She spent the afternoon with her sister and then joined the family for supper. When Elizabeth entered the drawing room, Miss Bingley frowned and turned away without speaking. Mr. Darcy's expression gave Elizabeth pause. She wondered what Miss Bingley had done. Caroline, knowing that she had not yet improved Darcy's opinion of her handling of their ill guest, placed a smile on her face and asked, "How is dear Miss Bennet? Is she much improved?"

Elizabeth knew that Caroline's interest was insincere, mainly because she kept her eyes on Mr. Darcy, but she answered politely. "Jane's fever has fortunately subsided, but she is weak and suffering from a sore throat and a headache. It is kind of you to ask."

"I do hope she will be well enough to return home soon. I am sure she will feel much better when restored to her family."

The rest had restored Elizabeth's sense of humor. "I must beg to differ, Miss Bingley. Jane is much better off in the quiet of Netherfield. However, we shall endeavor to not outstay our welcome."

Caroline's lips thinned in a frown. Before she could speak, Bingley said, "You are both welcome to stay as long as needed. You are delightful company and I hope to spend some time with Miss Bennet before she departs."

"Thank you, Mr. Bingley, you are most kind."

The butler announced dinner and Darcy stepped forward to offer his arm to Elizabeth. Bingley smiled at his friend, but Miss Bingley's lips nearly disappeared as her frown deepened. Seeing her look, Bingley offered his arm to his sister. He then led the others to the dining room.

Darcy pulled out Elizabeth's chair and seated her at the table. He took the chair beside hers, which was also next to Miss Bingley. Though his hostess attempted to dominate his conversation, Darcy frequently turned to Elizabeth to speak with her. Miss Bingley raised her voice slightly and spoke of the delights of the London season, knowing this topic would result in Miss Elizabeth's exclusion from the conversation. When the ladies left the gentlemen to their port, Elizabeth excused herself to check on Jane. She stayed away for thirty minutes to allow time for the men to return. Elizabeth had no desire to spend time alone with Miss Bingley and her sister. No doubt, they would spend their time looking down on her and speaking only to each other.

As the gentlemen crossed the hallway to rejoin the ladies, Darcy caught a flash of color from the corner of his eye. Looking up, he observed Elizabeth poised at the top of the stairs. Whispering something to Bingley, Darcy waited until the other gentlemen had continued on to the drawing room. Darcy moved to the bottom of the stairs and watched as Elizabeth descended. He held out his hand to her as she neared the bottom. Pausing on the last step, Elizabeth looked at her companion wonderingly.

"Is something the matter, Miss Elizabeth? Has Miss Bennet suffered a relapse?"

"No, Jane is well." She continued to look at him but did not speak further.

"Have I done something to offend you?" Darcy's confusion was growing.

"Not at all, Mr. Darcy."

"May I ask why you stare so?"

"I am sorry. I was just curious as to your purpose."

"My purpose?"

"I am aware that you are not fond of Miss Bingley. However, I cannot help but wonder if you are using my presence to send her a message."

Darcy studied her searchingly. "Do you find my attentions officious?"

"Not in the least, sir, unless they are only for show."

"I can assure you that is not the case."

"I am only concerned, Mr. Darcy, because Miss Bingley's anger mounts each time she sees your attention to me. I am a guest in her house and I do not wish to antagonize her when she is extending me hospitality."

"I do not wish to make you uncomfortable, Miss Elizabeth, but I will not pretend an interest in her that is not there, nor will I ignore you to save her feelings. I never gave the woman reason to believe I will offer for her."

Elizabeth nodded her understanding. "I am very pleased with your friendship, sir, and would welcome the opportunity to know you better. However, despite Miss Bingley's behavior, I would not wish to cause her unnecessary pain."

Darcy took Elizabeth by the hand and led her down the hall to Bingley's study. They stepped inside and stood behind the open door. Taking her other hand in his, Darcy asked, "Do you think we know one another well enough that I might request a courtship?"

"Are you sure you are ready for such a step, sir? Are you prepared to accept my mother as part of your family? If we move forward, will we be able to retain our friendship if things do not work out?

I would not wish to lose your friendship, sir, as I have come to value it greatly." Elizabeth's cheeks blushed at the forwardness of her words, but she did not wish for any misunderstandings.

"I believe the risk to be more than worth it. You are a remarkable young lady and unlike anyone I have ever met. I believe we would be very happy together if things progress as I hope."

Elizabeth's blush deepened and her smile grew. "Then I am willing to accept your offer of courtship. However, sir, it may be best for us to wait until Jane's health improves, as my father may wish to remove me from Netherfield if we are in a courtship. Perhaps we can use some of the time while I am here to get to know each other better. It will be much easier to talk uninterrupted here than in my mother's parlor—though we will always have the option of walking out to enjoy some quiet time together when at Longbourn."

"That is an excellent suggestion. In addition, perhaps we can manage to meet when you take your morning walks."

"That is also a good idea, Mr. Darcy. Now, we should join the others. If you go now, I will wait several minutes before entering."

"I do not think that will be necessary, as I told Bingley I would wait to escort you."

"So, Mr. Bingley is aware that we were alone all this time?" Elizabeth's face flushed with embarrassment.

"There is no need for embarrassment, Miss Elizabeth."

"This is exactly the kind of thing I wish to avoid with Miss Bingley."

"Are you telling me that you cannot deal with the likes of the Miss Bingleys of the world? I was counting on those abilities to help you when you face the ton for the first time." Darcy did not try to hide the grin that covered his face.

"You should know, Mr. Darcy, that my courage always rises with every attempt to intimidate."

"In that case." Darcy offered his arm to Elizabeth. They exited the office on their way to the drawing room.

"Ah, Mr. Darcy, there you are. What kept you from joining us. . ." Miss Bingley's cloying voice trailed off as she noticed Elizabeth on his arm. "Miss Eliza, if you need something, the proper thing to do is ask your hostess. You should not be bothering Mr. Darcy with your petty concerns."

"I am well aware of that fact, Miss Bingley. However, I saw no need to consult you as to whether I should accept the gentleman's arm when offered."

"Tell me, Miss Eliza, do you linger in the hall waiting to jump out at Mr. Darcy to force him to offer his arm?"

"Indeed not, Miss Bingley, but at least I wait for the arm to be offered."

Caroline's face turned red. Darcy could practically see the steam escaping her ears. The wheels turned as Miss Bingley attempted to form a scathing reply. Before she could recover, Charles spoke. "She has you there, Caroline. Poor Darcy. You clutch onto his arm the minute he arrives or enters a room and cling like a vine. The polite thing to do is to wait for him to offer."

"You exaggerate, Charles, as usual. I'm sure our dear friend does not mind my attention." Though he tried to disguise it, Darcy's grunt of disgust reached Miss Bingley's ears. She looked at the gentleman and caught him rolling his eyes. Caroline could not miss his dislike of her actions. Startled by his expression, Caroline blurted out, "Why did you not say something, Mr. Darcy?"

"As Miss Bennet said, it is appropriate to wait until offered. When I attempted to withdraw, you would cling tighter rather than understand my desire. I did not speak because I did not wish to offend Charles by correcting your behavior. He is the head of the family and that is his responsibility."

Caroline's voice and posture were rigid when she replied. "You have my apologies, sir. I shall attempt to refrain from such behavior in the future."

"I am glad this occurred, as I have tried to tell you this before, Caroline. However, you chose not to believe me." Miss Bingley glared at her brother as he spoke.

Mrs. Hurst felt sorry for her sister and spoke up, changing the subject. "How about some music? Miss Elizabeth, would you please play for us?"

Though Elizabeth knew that Miss Bingley deserved to be corrected, she would not have wished for her to be publically humiliated. Consequently, she agreed to play. Darcy escorted her to the pianoforte and offered to turn the pages for her. Elizabeth looked through the music and selected one with which she was quite familiar. She finished to polite applause, then surrendered her place to Mrs. Hurst. Miss Bingley was the last to play and chose several pieces. It was apparent that she knew them well, for she had no music in front of her. However, the changing expressions on her face made it clear to her audience that she was pondering her previous behavior and the things that had been said.

When Caroline finished playing, she retired for the night. Not long after her disappearance, Elizabeth excused herself, saying she would check on Jane before she retired. Since Mr. Hurst was the only one interested in playing cards, the Hursts soon retired. Darcy and Bingley retired to Bingley's study to enjoy a brandy before retiring.

"I hope you are not displeased with what I said to your sister," Darcy said.

"Not at all. I think this is the first time Caroline understood what I have been telling her for years."

"If it means she will no longer hang on my arm whenever she is near, I will be delighted with the outcome."

"Only time will tell. However, I imagine a cleared throat or meaningful glare will remind Caroline of the discussion until she learns to change her ways."

"I can only hope," replied Darcy. They quietly sipped their brandies before bidding each other goodnight. Thinking of his upcoming courtship and where it might lead, Darcy dreamed of Elizabeth that night for the first time.

# THINGS ARE LOOKING UP

WILLIAM OPENED THE LETTER FROM HIS sister with a sense of eagerness. Did his letter break through Georgiana's sadness and help her on the road to recovery.

*Pemberley*
*Derbyshire*
*8 November 1811*

*Dear William,*

*Your last letter was a delightful surprise. Thank you so much for the beautiful gifts. Please extend my thanks to the Bennet sisters for their assistance and excellent taste. Everything was very much to my liking. I am especially pleased with the journal and for the suggestion on its use. Having written in it daily since its arrival, I must agree that the journal makes a great confidante when one lacks a real person with whom to speak. Expressing my feelings in writing has also allowed me to be more open with Mrs. Annesley. Her input and experience have greatly helped me understand why I responded as I did.*

*I was thrilled with your descriptions of the Bennet sisters. I wish that such a family lived near Pemberley. Having so many friends close by would be thrilling. I believe that we would affect one another in positive ways. I hope that someday I shall be able to meet them. As they do not live close, perhaps we might correspond, which would increase my circle of acquaintances.*

*I am not sure if I ever thanked you for saving me from such a disastrous future. My feelings at the time were overwhelming and it took me some time to accept the loss of the loving family and home I thought would be mine. I am grateful that you arrived in time to save me from myself. Having had only each other, I thought my future would include a home filled with family. In the future, I would ask that you be open with me rather than always try to protect me. My recent experiences have opened my eyes to the world. I believe that I can handle any information, no matter how unpleasant.*

*I love you brother dear and look forward to being reunited for Christmas.*

*Affectionately,*
*Georgiana*

Darcy smiled as he refolded the letter and tucked it into his inner pocket. When he returned to his chambers, he would place this with his other correspondence from Georgiana. He was delighted to learn that Elizabeth's journal had been a success. Perhaps Elizabeth would consider corresponding with Georgiana once their courtship became official. Darcy had always desired that the woman he married and his dear sister would become the best of friends.

Undoubtedly, Georgiana required a woman close to her in age to confide in and help her grow in confidence as she prepared for her coming out in a few years.

He hoped he would have an opportunity to share Georgiana's letter with Elizabeth later in the day. Thinking of the two ladies he held most dear, Darcy could see a bright future before him. Knowing that he wished to see this courtship through to its natural end, he considered making a quick trip to London when Elizabeth and Miss Bennet returned home, to get his solicitor started on the marriage settlement. Darcy wished to make haste when the time to propose was at hand. He could not help but wonder if he would be engaged—perhaps even married—by the end of the year. With a smile on his face, Darcy exited and headed for the dining room for the midday meal. As he reached the bottom of the stairs, Elizabeth descended from Jane's room.

"Ah, Miss Elizabeth, well met. I received a letter from Georgiana today. She asked me particularly to extend to you her thanks for the journal and the suggestion that it can serve as an excellent confidant. She has been writing daily since receiving it and indicated that the journal has helped her to organize her thoughts and feelings. It has also helped her open up to her companion and learn from Mrs. Annesley's wisdom."

"I am delighted to hear that and so pleased that my gift helped your sister."

"I have a favor to ask of you, Miss Elizabeth. Once our courtship is approved by your father, might you be willing to correspond with my sister? I think it would be a great way for the two of you to get to know one another before you meet. I also think corresponding with you would be a great benefit for Georgie, as she would have a real person, close to her in age, in whom to confide."

"I would be happy to do so. It would be a delight to correspond with someone whose life and experiences differ from mine as well as to be of service to your sister."

Darcy grinned and offered his arm to Elizabeth. They entered the dining room with smiling faces. Miss Bingley's features remained impassive as she greeted the new arrivals. Caroline's behavior had been much subdued since the second night of Miss Elizabeth's arrival. She had been disturbed to learn of Mr. Darcy's opinion of her but was loath to allow a country miss like Miss Eliza Bennet to succeed with such a prominent gentleman where she had failed entirely. While she pretended to be accepting of the situation, Caroline pondered whether she could do something about it.

It was after dinner on the fifth day of Elizabeth's stay at Netherfield. Jane was much improved and made her first appearance in the drawing room after the midday meal. Bingley rushed to her side as she entered the room leaning on Elizabeth's arm. Upon offering his arm to Jane, he escorted her to a chair near the fire, then placed a blanket over her lap. Jane had been glad for his strong arm, as she felt a bit unsteady on her feet after having spent so many days in bed. After ensuring that Jane had a cup of tea, Bingley devoted his attention and conversation to his "angel."

Darcy and Elizabeth also enjoyed a quiet conversation, though both caught themselves smiling at the other couple. Delight filled Elizabeth at the attention the amiable gentleman showed her dearest sister. After about thirty minutes, the two couples drifted towards one another and the conversation became a bit more animated.

The many conversations in the room were interrupted when Bingley cried out, "I want to give a ball." Little did he know that his words would cause such an outcry.

"What a lovely idea, Mr. Bingley," said Jane softly.

"I am sure the neighborhood will enjoy a ball," added Elizabeth.

"Charles, you cannot be serious! I doubt the items that would be needed can even be obtained in a village such as this. I will not do it."

"Then perhaps Louisa will arrange things for me and act as my hostess."

"I do hope you will, Mrs. Hurst. I believe even I might enjoy a ball here at Netherfield."

At Darcy's words, Caroline Bingley's mouth fell open. She could not remember a time when Mr. Darcy had enjoyed a social occasion. "Well, if Louisa is willing to help, I suppose it might be possible to make the necessary arrangements," Caroline said.

Bingley knew precisely why Caroline's opinion had changed, but he had previously decided to no longer bow to her whims. He was tired of the fuss and bother she always created when she did not get her way or when she did not wish to comply with another's wishes. "No,

Caroline, I am sure that Louisa can manage. If she should require assistance, I am sure that the eldest Misses Bennet would be willing to help."

"Of course," said Jane.

"We would be happy to help if you desire it, Mrs. Hurst." Elizabeth noticed that Miss Bingley's anger was increasing. Fortunately, Mrs. Hurst did not seem opposed to the idea of arranging a ball or to the assistance of Elizabeth and Jane.

"What day shall we set for it?" wondered Bingley. "Of course, we must wait until Miss Bennet is thoroughly recovered. We could not possibly host a ball if she were unable to attend." Jane blushed at Bingley's words, but a small smile graced her features.

"I believe that Jane should be completely recovered within a week, or so Mr. Jones stated. Perhaps in two weeks would be a good time," suggested Elizabeth.

"Obviously, Miss Eliza, you know nothing about what goes into planning a true society event. Two weeks might be sufficient for the type of events to which you are accustomed, but not for the type of events that one would see in the ton." Caroline's tone dripped with disdain. Her gaze was haughty and, if possible, her nose was farther in the air than usual.

"It surprises me to hear you say that, Miss Bingley," Darcy said. "My staff, and even my Aunt Lady Matlock, would not have a problem with having two weeks to arrange a ball. Of course, Mrs. Hurst has not complained about the time; perhaps she is more experienced."

Caroline Bingley looked indignant at Mr. Darcy's words, while Louisa Hurst bowed her head to hide a smile. Caroline's mouth popped open, but no words came out of it. She clamped her mouth closed and folded her arms over her thin chest as she turned to stare out the window. She determined her course of action. Caroline would force Louisa to accept her opinions and thus ensure that the Bennet sisters played no part in the planning and would receive no praise for their efforts.

"Two weeks would be approximately the twenty-sixth of November. Shall we set the date for then?" offered Charles. Everyone except Miss Bingley nodded their agreement. Jane did not remain downstairs long after the date was determined. Despite wanting to participate in the discussion about the ball, Elizabeth caught Jane attempting to hide a yawn.

When Elizabeth returned from helping Jane to her chamber, Mrs. Hurst sat with Mr. Bingley and Mr. Darcy. She joined them and the planning for the ball began. Whenever Elizabeth offered an opinion or suggestion, a derisive snort or muttered, imprecation came from where Miss Bingley sat thumbing through the newest ladies' magazine. She was generally ignored as Mrs. Hurst began making a list of things to be done.

"I believe we should check with Mrs. Webster to ensure she will have time to make enough white soup for the supper." Bingley, who sat nearest, pulled the bell to summon the housekeeper. When Mrs. Dawson entered, Louisa said, "We plan to hold a ball on the twenty-sixth of November. Do you think that will allow Mrs. Webster enough time to make white soup? If not, please notify me immediately."

"Certainly, Mrs. Hurst." The housekeeper turned to exit but paused at the sound of Mr. Bingley's voice.

"Mrs. Dawson, please discuss all issues relating to the ball only with Mrs. Hurst. Miss Bingley feels a bit under the weather and we do not wish to burden her with the responsibilities of planning the ball. We need her to rest so that she can attend the event."

"Of course, Mr. Bingley. I will discuss things exclusively with Mrs. Hurst." Only after the housekeeper left the room did she allow a smile to appear on her face. Undoubtedly, Miss Bingley was being difficult and her brother's actions would prohibit her from interfering. Mrs. Dawson intended to ensure that the entire staff knew of Mr. Bingley's directive.

After breakfast the next day, Jane joined the others downstairs. Mrs. Hurst greeted her warmly. Along with Elizabeth, the ladies settled to discuss the arrangements for the ball. Miss Bingley lurked nearby, listening to a discussion about the menu for the dinner that would take place during the ball. Occasionally, she offered a suggestion, such as, "Do not forget to include Mr. Darcy's favorite dishes. You would not wish to insult our dear friend." Mrs. Hurst acknowledged the words with a nod, then continued her conversation as though her sister had not interrupted.

Jane joined the family for dinner and the discussion turned to when the Bennet sisters would return home. "I will write and ask Papa to send the carriage tomorrow," said Elizabeth.

"There is no need for you to rush off," replied Bingley. "You yourself said that Miss Bennet's recovery would be best at Netherfield.

We would not want to rush her and have her relapse." Bingley addressed those words to Elizabeth, then turned to Jane. "You must be fully recovered, Miss Bennet, because I would like to take this opportunity to request your first two dances at the ball."

Jane blushed becomingly at his request. "I am delighted to accept your kind offer, Mr. Bingley."

The grinding of Miss Bingley's teeth was almost audible to those nearby as she forced herself to not make a derogatory remark. A false smile quickly replaced her grimace as her expression turned from annoyed to cunning.

"Do you plan to follow my brother's excellent example as well, sir? You indicated you would enjoy a ball. Surely, you will honor your host by dancing?"

"Indeed, I do," agreed Darcy. Miss Bingley's smile grew and she gave Elizabeth a condescendingly smug glare. Darcy turned his back on Caroline. In his deep, resonant voice, he asked, "Miss Elizabeth, would you do me the great honor of accepting my hand for the first two dances?"

"Yes, Mr. Darcy. I thank you for your kind offer."

Again, Caroline's mouth flapped open before she descended into angry silence. *What is wrong with Mr. Darcy*, she wondered. *He has changed considerably since we arrived in this little hamlet. I shall need to persuade Charles that we must get Mr. Darcy away from here for his own good. We would not wish to be blamed if he made an unsuitable and unwise choice of wife. If we allowed that to happen, Lady Matlock could ruin me in society.* Then Caroline had another thought. *Perhaps I should send an invitation to the Matlocks with a word of caution.* Despite her displeasure with Mr. Darcy's behavior, a satisfied smile appeared on her face, causing everyone to wonder what scheme Caroline was concocting.

Later that afternoon, while Jane was resting between meals, Elizabeth happened upon the gentlemen. "I am sorry to report that my mother says the carriage will not be available for several days. Perhaps we might borrow a carriage to return us home?"

Darcy and Bingley looked at each other before speaking. Neither gentleman truly wanted the ladies to depart. "Might I make a suggestion?" asked Darcy. "Perhaps you ladies would accompany us to church tomorrow. Then I could return you home and speak to your father, Miss Elizabeth. Would that suit?"

"We gratefully accept your offer, sir."

Bingley cast a confused glance at his friend, wondering why Darcy would need to speak with Mr. Bennet. His confusion cleared when he saw the tender smile that Darcy and Miss Elizabeth shared. Bingley would have to make a point of talking to his friend before addressing Miss Bennet later in the day.

# TWO COURTSHIPS BEGIN

THE ARRIVAL OF THE BINGLEY AND Darcy carriages at the Meryton church on Sunday morning caused a great stir. As his vehicle led the procession, Mr. Darcy stepped down first and handed out Miss Elizabeth Bennet. They were followed by Mr. Bingley, who assisted Miss Jane Bennet. Each gentleman offered an arm to his companion and escorted her into the house of worship. When the couples entered, they noticed the Bennet family taking their seats. The gentlemen escorted the ladies to their family pew, where Mr. Darcy spoke briefly to Mr. Bennet. Mrs. Bennet could not make out what was said but hated to lose the gentlemen's company so soon. Consequently, the Bennet matron invited the gentlemen to join the family for Sunday dinner. Bingley was quick to accept the invitation for them both before the gentlemen took their seats across the aisle from the lovely Jane and Elizabeth.

The members of the congregation enjoyed the unexpected performance that came with the service. The families from Longbourn and Netherfield Park both sat in the first pew due to the fact that they were the largest estates in the area. Seated on the aisle directly across from each other, the four young people all tried to focus on the service, but occasionally heads would turn ever so slightly and eyes would stray either right or left. If the minister moved to one side of the altar or the other, the two young couples had an excuse to stare to their hearts' content. When the service was over, the gentlemen quickly stepped into the nave and offered their arms to the ladies, leading them out of the church. Bingley whispered to his sister that they would not be joining the family for dinner. Darcy and his friend assisted the ladies into the carriage and headed towards Longbourn.

As the carriage traversed the short distance to the young ladies' home, Darcy spoke. "I need to make a short trip to town to attend to a little business. I will leave early tomorrow morning and return in time to call on Friday afternoon."

At Darcy's first words, Elizabeth felt a sense of loss that surprised her, but the sensation ebbed as he spoke of returning before the end of the week. "I will miss you, sir. I believe we should not announce our relationship until you return."

"You do not wish to announce our courtship?" The hurt in Darcy's tone was obvious.

"You misunderstand, sir. I wish to announce it when you are present to share in the joy. It would be awkward having to explain why you are away when news of the announcement begins to spread."

Darcy appeared mollified, but he worried that someone else might swoop in and steal Elizabeth while he was away. Not wishing Elizabeth to know of his concerns, he teased, "I hope you will not allow another gentleman to sweep you off your feet while I am away."

Elizabeth's initial reaction was to laugh, but something in the tightness of his jaw and the expression in his eyes alerted her to his true feelings. "You have nothing to worry about, Mr. Darcy. No one in Meryton has taken note of me for the last twenty years; I seriously doubt that will change in a few short days."

After a delicious meal, the ladies departed, leaving the gentlemen to their port. As soon as the door closed behind both the ladies and the servants, Darcy took the opportunity to speak.

"Mr. Bennet, I greatly admire your daughter, Miss Elizabeth. Just before the ladies' departure from Netherfield, I asked her for permission for a courtship. I am delighted to say that she accepted me. I hope you will grant your permission, sir."

Studying the young man before him, Mr. Bennet considered not only the gentleman's words but what he had observed of his daughter's behavior. Elizabeth's affection for the young man was evident when they had entered the church together that morning. "What do you expect from this courtship, sir?"

Darcy studied the gentleman before him, wondering what he meant. However, Darcy could not be anything but himself, which was evident in his reply. "I expect this to progress to its natural conclusion. I hope it will not be too long before Miss Elizabeth accepts my hand in marriage. I am sure of my feelings, sir, but a young lady as remarkable as Miss Elizabeth deserves to be courted and wooed properly. I will always ensure that she is happy and give her everything her heart might desire."

The strength of Darcy's feelings was evident in his words and tone. Mr. Bennet did not doubt the young man would do exactly what he said. "I am happy to give you my permission, Mr. Darcy, and I look forward to knowing you better."

The smile which graced Darcy's face showed his dimples. So startled was Mr. Bennet that he almost missed the words Darcy spoke.

"May I make one last request, sir?" At Mr. Bennet's nod, Darcy continued. "Miss Elizabeth would like to hold off on the pronouncement of our courtship until the end of the week. You see, I need to make a quick trip to London for business. I will depart early tomorrow and return in time to call on Friday afternoon."

"Very well, Mr. Darcy. I will wait to make the announcement. But you realize, sir, that you are forcing me to endure Mrs. Bennet's effusions twice, as I have a suspicion that Mr. Bingley wishes to make a similar request of me." Mr. Bennet glanced at the other young gentleman, who blushed from the roots of his hair to the tips of his ears but nodded his agreement. "Well, then, Mr. Bingley, what request did you wish to make of me?"

Tugging his waistcoat down and running a finger around the inside of his cravat, Bingley began. "I would like to request your permission to court Miss Jane Bennet. We spoke this morning and she accepted as well."

"You, also, have my permission, Mr. Bingley. Did you wish to announce it now or wait for Mr. Darcy and make the announcements at the same time?"

"There is no need to wait, sir."

"Should we join the ladies, then, and share the good news?"

The younger gentlemen arose with alacrity and hurried across the hall to join the ladies. While Darcy took his seat, Mr. Bennet prevented Bingley from leaving his side while beckoning to his eldest daughter. "It gives me great pleasure to announce that Mr. Bingley has requested a courtship with our Jane, and I gave my permission."

Mrs. Bennet's shrill squeal of pleasure caused Darcy to start. Elizabeth looked at him with concern and a touch of embarrassment. Rather than cause Elizabeth any undue stress, he broke into a grin. Elizabeth smiled back. Leaning in close to Darcy's ear, she whispered, "Now you know what to expect when Mama learns of our arrangement." Darcy's eyes widened, but he did not speak. Elizabeth's soft giggle reached him and he knew it was in response to his surprised expression.

"Are you not curious as to what your father said to my request?" Darcy's expression was so severe that Elizabeth felt a flutter of fear.

"Papa agreed, did he not? If he did not, I should be forced to change his mind."

Darcy smiled at her words before discreetly squeezing Elizabeth's hand. "That will not be necessary. Though I am delighted to know that you would fight for our relationship, if necessary." Darcy gave Elizabeth his dimpled smile, which grew as he saw a deep blush suffuse her face.

The gentlemen stayed as long as politeness allowed. When it was time for them to depart, Mrs. Bennet requested that her two eldest daughters escort the gentlemen to the door. As Elizabeth passed her mother, Mrs. Bennet clutched her arm and hissed, "Keep Mr. Darcy out of the way to allow Jane and Mr. Bingley a proper goodbye." When she finished speaking, she gave Elizabeth a little shove to hurry her along.

Jane and Elizabeth watched from the steps as the carriage started down the driveway. When it turned out of the gates and was no longer in sight,

Elizabeth and Jane pulled their shawls tighter about them and locked arms. They strolled to the walled park and took a seat on a bench in the sunshine.

"How do you feel now that you are in an acknowledged courtship?" Elizabeth asked her elder sister and dearest friend.

"Oh, Lizzy! It feels wonderful! I never dreamed I would meet someone like Mr. Bingley. He is everything I have wished for since we were little girls. How about you, Lizzy? Papa gave his permission for your courtship as well."

"I am very excited about getting to spend more time with Mr. Darcy. However, even this early in our relationship, we seem to share an unusually close connection. I find myself missing him already. I never expected to find a man who would accept me for who I am. Mr. Darcy likes my quick mind and pert opinions, and I truly enjoy having someone intelligent enough to debate. I feel very blessed that Mr. Bingley leased Netherfield Park and brought his good friend with him."

"We are indeed the luckiest girls in the world," said Jane. The sisters fell into each other's arms for a warm embrace before collapsing into giggles. When they regained control of their laughter, they strolled arm and arm back to the house and up to their rooms.

# PRIMING THE PARSON

THE NEXT MORNING AT BREAKFAST, MR. Bennet said to his wife, "I hope you have ordered a good dinner for today, as we will have a guest joining us."

"Oooh," cried Mrs. Bennet. "Is Mr. Bingley joining us? I shall have to order an additional course for dinner."

"It is not Mr. Bingley, though it would not surprise me to see him here today. It is, in fact, a gentleman known to us only by name. I received a letter from my cousin and heir, Mr. Collins, informing me that he will be arriving today and will stay for a fortnight."

"I shall certainly not serve a better meal for that thief. How dare he invite himself to visit! He probably wishes to count the silver and take inventory of the house. Oh, how I hate that man."

"You might wish to reserve your opinion, madam. In his letter, Mr. Collins indicates he intends to offer an olive branch and hopes to find a wife among our daughters."

"Oh, that is wonderful. With Jane in a courtship, Elizabeth will be the perfect match for Mr. Collins. Then I shall be able to remain in my home when you are dead, Mr. Bennet."

"No, Mrs. Bennet. Elizabeth would not be a good match for Mr. Collins. Our daughter is far too intelligent for a simple country parson."

"And whose fault is that? I told you it was a waste of time to educate her so. Elizabeth will need to learn to hold her tongue and learn her place as Mr. Collins' wife."

"Mrs. Bennet, I forbid you to put Elizabeth forward as a wife for Mr. Collins. I made another arrangement for Lizzy, which I will announce at the end of the week. So, as you can see, Elizabeth is not available either." Mrs. Bennet looked at her husband doubtfully. She could not decide whether Mr. Bennet meant what he said or was trying to protect his favorite daughter.

"Well, my Lydia is too good for him, so I guess Kitty will have to do," said Mrs. Bennet carelessly.

"I do not wish to marry a parson," whined Kitty. "I want to marry an officer in a red coat."

"Oh, hush, Kitty. You will do as you are told."

Kitty burst into tears and ran from the table to the sound of her younger sister's laughter.

"Mama," said Jane, ever the peacemaker. "I think Kitty might be too young to handle the responsibilities that would come with being Mr. Collins' wife. A parson's wife should be familiar with the scriptures and knowledgeable in music in case she must play for the congregation."

"That is true," said Elizabeth. "She should be mature, of a serious nature, and capable of helping those in her husband's parish."

Mrs. Bennet looked at her daughters as if they had lost their senses. "Why on earth would a man wish to marry such a boring creature?"

"Such behavior is not boring to a man with a parson's responsibilities. She is the perfect helpmate for someone in Mr. Collins' position," said Jane soothingly. "Surely with your wide acquaintance, you can think of someone who possesses those qualities?"

Mrs. Bennet was confused by Jane's words. She looked around at the others at the table with her as though hoping to understand what Jane wanted from her. It was then that her eyes fell on her middle daughter. Mary's head was bowed over her book of sermons and she did not see the gleam in her mother's eyes, though both Jane and Elizabeth knew that her mother understood what they were trying to tell her. Mr. Bennet regarded the scene with a sardonic grin.

When Mrs. Bennet began shaking her head, he feared what thoughtless words might come from her mouth. Speaking before his wife had the chance to do so, he addressed his middle daughter. "Mary, Mrs. Johnson is feeling poorly, and I asked Mrs. Hill to prepare a basket for the family. Would you please deliver it to her right away?"

"Of course, Papa. I shall alert Mrs. Hill that I am ready to perform the errand before fetching my cloak and bonnet. That will give her time to put in any final items."

Mr. Bennet followed his daughter from the room and closed the door tightly behind him. Fortunately, the door muffled the sound of Mrs. Bennet's wail.

"But, Mr. Collins will never choose the plainest of my daughters. What shall we do? He will pick someone else and we shall be thrown from our home to starve in the hedgerows." Mrs. Bennet's words ended on a sob as she fluttered her handkerchief in the air.

Jane and Elizabeth exchanged a look. "You go and rest until Mr. Collins arrives, Mama. Leave Mary to Lizzy and me. We shall even enlist the aid of Kitty and Lydia to ensure that Mary shines as the loveliest of the Bennet daughters during Mr. Collins' visit."

Jane and Elizabeth assisted their mother to her room and then turned down the hallway to solicit their younger sisters helping with Mary's transformation. Elizabeth knocked on the door, then opened it when Lydia laughingly called, "Enter."

When Kitty saw her elder sisters, she moaned, "I do not want to marry Mr. Collins!"

"You will not have to marry Mr. Collins if you both help us with a little project."

"Oooh, what is it?" asked Lydia, always eager to engage in anything that seemed to offer a bit of excitement.

Jane and Elizabeth filled them in on the plan to turn the plainest of the Bennet sisters into the resident beauty. The sisters discussed a wardrobe and hairstyles that would best suit Mary. They also knew they would have to convince Mary to go along with the plan.

When Mary returned from visiting the Johnsons, one of Longbourn's tenant families, she made her way up the stairs to rest in her room. She was surprised to find Jane and Elizabeth waiting within.

"Jane, what are you and Lizzy doing in my room? Is anything wrong?"

Her eldest sisters looked at one another. With a nod from Jane, Elizabeth spoke. "Mary, were you listening to what Papa was saying at breakfast this morning?"

"I believe he said Mr. Collins planned to visit."

"And you do realize who Mr. Collins is, do you not?"

"He is Papa's heir."

"Yes. Did you hear what else Papa said about him?"

"No, what else is there?"

"Mr. Collins is looking to marry one of us so that we will not be homeless upon Papa's death," Jane said. Mary looked at them without understanding. "Well, you know that I am courting Mr. Bingley."

Mary nodded.

"And can you keep a secret?" questioned Elizabeth. Mary was surprised that her sister wished to share a confidence with her, but nodded her agreement. "I am courting Mr. Darcy. Papa has given his approval, but we will not announce it until he returns at the end of the week. From what Papa has shared, Mr. Collins is a very formal gentleman. He will wish to marry the oldest available daughter so as not to cause hurt feelings."

Mary looked at her sisters as understanding dawned. "You think he will wish to marry me?" Her tone and expression were both filled with doubt.

"You are the most logical choice. If he is a man of sense, he will wish to marry you. Jane and I are both unavailable, and Lydia and Kitty are far too young and immature to be a parson's wife. With your love of sermons and your talent with the tenants, I believe you would make an excellent parson's wife."

"But Mr. Collins will never look at me with the four of you around. I know that I am the least attractive of the Bennet sisters. I have heard it often enough from Mama."

"If you will trust us, we will ensure that Mr. Collins will find you the loveliest of the available girls."

"What do you mean 'trust you?' You know that Mr. Fordyce's sermons say that vanity is a sin."

Having prepared for this situation, Elizabeth replied, "Vanity is a sin only when carried to the extreme. It is not wrong to look one's best. That is all we are suggesting. Allow us to help you look your best."

Mary looked doubtful but eventually agreed. Lizzy rang the bell. When the maid responded, she requested a bathtub and hot water. Mary's eyes widened, but she did not speak, as Jane was already pulling the pins from her hair while Elizabeth was assisting with the buttons down the back of Mary's gown. The water, prepared in advance, was being delivered by the time the girls had Mary in her dressing gown.

Before she knew it, Mary was in the tub and Jane was washing her hair as Elizabeth rushed to the door to answer a knock. In bustled Kitty and Lydia with a gown and several colors of ribbons.

"I also brought some of my honeysuckle water to add to the bath and to use in rinsing Mary's hair."

"That was very thoughtful of you, Kitty, and an excellent idea."

Elizabeth took the bottle from her sister. She added a few drops to the bath water and to the bucket on the hearth, which they would use to rinse Mary's hair. When she was out of the tub, Lydia dragged Mary to sit before the fire and began rubbing her hair with a towel. Kitty had scrubbed her sister's nails in the tub. She now smoothed Mary's nails with a mixture of cinnabar and emery, then wiped them with a bit of oil to soften them and make them shine.

With Mary's hair now dry, Elizabeth brushed it until it shone. Then Jane began to section the hair and braid it, twisting and pinning it into a soft, pretty style. Jane fashioned a couple of loose curls next to Mary's face as Elizabeth removed her glasses.

"You need these only to read, so I think it would be best to keep them in your pocket unless you need them," suggested Elizabeth as she tucked the glasses into the pocket of Mary's dress.

Just then the crunch of wheels on gravel reached their ears. They rushed to the window and saw a small trap stopping before the house. A tall, skinny gentleman stepped down. They could not discern his features, as his parson's hat blocked the view.

Not giving Mary an opportunity to see her changed look, Jane said, "Mary, would you please go down and join Mama to greet our guests? We must change before we join you."

Mary looked doubtful, but her sisters smiled encouragingly. "Of course, Jane. I will see you all shortly."

As the sound of Mary's footsteps receded, Elizabeth looked at the younger girls and asked, "Do you remember what you are supposed to do?"

"Yes, Lizzy. We are to be complimentary to Mary and show no interest in Mr. Collins," said Kitty.

"Who would be interested in a boring parson?" asked Lydia with a laugh.

Jane and Elizabeth rolled their eyes as they shooed their younger sisters downstairs to join the others. The older girls then looked at one another and shook their heads before hurrying to change and join the rest of their family.

As Elizabeth and Jane approached the sitting room, the rather monotone voice of a stranger reached them. "I have heard much of the loveliness of your daughters, Mrs. Bennet, particularly the eldest. Miss Bennet is said to be of unparalleled beauty. It is hard to imagine there could be more beauty than that arrayed before me." The sisters could hear the twittering giggles of Lydia and Kitty.

"My Jane is beautiful, so it will not surprise you to learn that a gentleman from the neighborhood is courting her," offered Mrs. Bennet.

Mr. Collins cast a sharp look at Mrs. Bennet. "I was not aware that any of your daughters was being courted."

Her tone harsh, Mrs. Bennet huffed, "As you have never visited us, how could you be aware of anything concerning my daughters?"

"I stopped in the village to ask for directions to the estate. The owner of the general store was very forthcoming with information about your family."

Mrs. Bennet merely sniffed in reply.

"Odious man," muttered Lizzy before turning to her sister. "In spite of your beauty, you are safe, as the family is aware of your courtship. Let us hope that my appearance will keep him from developing an interest in me and turn his attention to Mary, who is the best choice he could make among his cousins."

Jane and Elizabeth entered the room. Their appearance was met with a variety of reactions. Jane appeared as she always did, so it was Elizabeth who drew attention.

# LIZZY IN DISGUISE

MRS. BENNET'S JAW DROPPED WHEN SHE saw her second daughter enter the sitting room. Initially, her mouth flopped open and closed as she gaped at her daughter. "Lizzy," she began, an expression of irritation on her face, as she had hoped to turn their cousin's interest to her second daughter. As Mr. Collins stared at the new additions to the party, Jane and Elizabeth held their breaths, hoping their mother would not say anything to ruin their plans. Fortunately, Lydia, who was seated next to her mother, leaned in quickly and whispered to her. What Mrs. Bennet learned caused her to pause. Her mouth flapped again, but she said nothing, as she realized it did not matter which of her daughters became the next mistress of Longbourn. In fact, she might more easily dominate Mary than Elizabeth and would not need to give up her position as the estate's mistress until her death.

Finally, Mrs. Bennet spoke. "Mr. Collins, allow me to introduce my eldest daughter, Miss Jane Bennet, and my second daughter, Miss Elizabeth Bennet."

Mr. Collins practically salivated at the sight of Jane. He attempted to take Jane's hand, intending to kiss the back of it, but Elizabeth linked her arm through her sister's to prevent this as Jane hurriedly bent her other arm behind her waist. Not to be thwarted in showing his adoration to Jane, the gentleman bowed deeply, though his eyes went no lower than her bosom. "My dear cousin Jane, I am overwhelmed by your beauty. I knew that I should find the perfect companion for my future life here amongst my cousins. Now I know I need look no further."

"Mr. Collins," said Mrs. Bennet with asperity, "I explained to you already that our neighbor, Mr. Bingley, is courting our Jane."

"A courtship is not an engagement, madam. Surely, my lovely cousin must be swayed by the opportunity to become the mistress of her childhood home upon the unfortunate demise of her dear father. What sensible woman would not desire such good fortune as I can offer?"

Elizabeth scowled at the way the clergyman stared at Jane's chest. At his ridiculous words, she looked at Jane and rolled her eyes, then squeezed Jane's hand encouragingly.

"I am sorry to disappoint you, Mr. Collins, but I willingly entered this courtship with my affections engaged. I could never break my word. I am afraid you will need to find your future companion from among my sisters." In spite of her gentle nature, Jane was not unintelligent. Obviously, Mr. Collins expected to ask for and receive whichever of his cousins he desired. It was also clear that he believed he deserved the most attractive of them all. To test her theory, Jane turned his attention to Elizabeth. "Perhaps you might prefer my next younger sister, Elizabeth. She is intelligent and witty and quite popular in the neighborhood. If not she, Mary is the next in order of age."

Reluctantly, Mr. Collins cast his eyes around the room, passing right over Elizabeth. "And which is Miss Elizabeth?"

"I am," Elizabeth answered in a whiny, high voice while trying to suppress her grin.

Mr. Collins turned toward the sound. What he saw was a short young woman in a drab brown dress. Her hair was pulled back in a tight bun; her expression was severe. A pair of Mary's old glasses was perched on the end of her nose.

Mr. Collins' brows rose in horror at the sight of the second Bennet daughter. With barely a nod in Lizzy's directions, Mr. Collins looked at the three remaining girls. "Which of my lov—cousins is Miss Mary?"

Mrs. Bennet recognized her opportunity, so she stepped in and began to brag about her middle child. "The one seated there is Mary. She is lovely, is she not?" Mrs. Bennet gave Mr. Collins the chance to examine her daughter before continuing to speak. "Mary is demure and spends a great deal of time reading the scriptures and studying Mr. Fordyce's sermons for young women. She also excels at the pianoforte. Mary helps with caring for our tenants and would be an asset to any clergyman and his parish." Mary blushed at her mother's unexpected praise and at the way Mr. Collins studied her.

Looking between the three girls, he had to make a choice. Lady Catherine had commanded him to come home with a wife from among his cousins. Mr. Collins would not fail his patroness. He desired Jane with fervency. In his mind, his pride of place as the clergyman to the great Lady Catherine de Bourgh entitled him to the most beautiful of women. However, Jane seemed committed to her courtship and Mr. Collins did not think he would be able to change her mind. The thought of Cousin Elizabeth was not to be borne. When she had first entered, Mr. Collins had thought her a maid and ignored her for the beauty at her side. Lady Catherine would not wish so unattractive a lady's presence in her drawing room. That left Cousin Mary. Though not the loveliest of the sisters, she was quite attractive and did indeed seem demure and like someone of whom Lady Catherine might approve.

Making his decision, Mr. Collins said, "Cousin Mary, perhaps you would tell me about your favorite section of Mr. Fordyce's book." He moved to sit in the chair next to that of the middle Bennet daughter. Kitty and Lydia moved to the table where they often sat and worked on redecorating their bonnets. Jane and Elizabeth soon joined them. The sisters shared a conspiratorial smile as they took up their needlework.

Mr. Collins and Mary spent a good portion of the afternoon in conversation. After dinner, Mrs. Bennet encouraged Mary to play the piano. At the urging of her elder sisters, she chose to play hymns, which they said would show Mr. Collins another way she could be of assistance in his parish. All in all, as the day ended, everyone was pleased with the way things had gone.

The next day, Mr. Collins, accompanied all of the Bennet sisters, except Elizabeth, who needed to maintain her disguise, into Meryton. Kitty and Lydia led the way, walking well in front of their sisters in the hopes that they might meet some of the officers before completing their errands. Mr. Collins offered an arm to both Mary and Jane. The eldest Bennet sister paused before accepting but could think of no reason to refuse. However, she looked down or away from the others as they walked along. Mr. Collins attempted to include her in the conversation, but after receiving nothing more than monosyllables, he devoted his attention to Mary.

By the time Mr. Collins and his companions had made their way onto the high street of Meryton, they discovered Lydia and Kitty in conversation with Lieutenant Denney and another gentleman whom they did not recognize. Jane dropped Mr. Collins' arm and rapidly approached her younger sisters. Placing a calming hand on each of their shoulders, Jane acknowledged Lieutenant Denney and waited for the gentleman to introduce his companion.

"Miss Bennet, Miss Mary, Miss Kitty, Miss Lydia, allow me to introduce Lieutenant George Wickham, who just enlisted in our militia unit and will be an excellent addition to our company."

"Indeed, he will," offered Lydia before she and Kitty dissolved into giggles.

The introductions were acknowledged. Then Jane introduced their cousin to the two officers. When he heard the name "Wickham," Mr. Collins looked askance at the gentleman. That name was familiar to him, but he could not recall why. In spite of the distraction, Mr. Collins bowed low to the gentlemen.

"Tell me, do you like to dance, Lieutenant Wickham?"

"What gentleman does not like to dance with partners as lovely as those before me? I hope there will be a dance soon so that I might enjoy a set with each of you." As all the young ladies smiled at the charming gentleman, Mr. Collins stepped closer to Mary in a show of possession. Shock showed on her face at the parson's actions.

It was at this moment that Mr. Bingley entered Meryton on his horse. Seeing the Bennet sisters, he trotted in the direction of the group. Upon dismounting at their side, Bingley took Jane's hand in his and bowed over it before acknowledging the rest of the group. After introducing Bingley to the unknown members of the party, the group remained in conversation for some few minutes.

Sitting in her usual spot before the window, where she could observe the comings and goings of the village, Mrs. Philips saw her nieces talking to a group of gentlemen. With her love of company, Mrs. Bennet's elder sister rushed from her home and invited the group to join her for tea.

As no one had anywhere particular to be, each accepted her invitation. Wickham listened to the conversations around him to learn what he could of those in the neighborhood. He noted the attention paid to two of the sisters by two of the gentlemen in the company. Wickham learned that Mr. Bingley had a well-dowered sister and that the second Bennet sister had not walked into the village with the group. He also discovered that Darcy had been in the area, but departed a few days earlier. That news brought a smile to Wickham's face. He only wondered which of the Bennet sisters would be most likely to believe his tale of woe and offer him sympathy and perhaps a few liberties.

As Wickham contemplated his choice, Mrs. Philips made a sudden decision that she immediately announced. "I believe I will hold a card party tomorrow evening and you all must come."

The youngest of her nieces were quick to accept, looking at Jane with pleading eyes. "I am sure we would be happy to join you, aunt, if Mama has no other plans," her eldest niece informed her.

"I am sorry," said Bingley, "but we have accepted an invitation to dine with the Gouldings." He looked at Jane as he spoke, a sad expression on his face.

"I am not on duty tomorrow evening," said Denney.

"As it will be my first full day with the militia, I am uncertain what my situation will be. However, I will make every effort to attend, as I would not wish to disappoint such delightful company," said Wickham.

"An evening of cards," said Mr. Collins. "I shall be pleased to attend. My esteemed patroness, Lady Catherine de Bourgh, often invites me to make a fourth for an evening of cards at her estate, Rosings Park."

A short time later, the party broke up, with everyone expressing their delight at being together again the next evening.

When the time for Mrs. Philips' card party arrived, everyone from the tea party with the exception of Mr. Bingley was in attendance. Again, Elizabeth remained at home to prevent Mr. Collins from discovering her actual appearance.

As the card party progressed, Mr. Wickham found the opportunity he sought and took a seat next to Miss Kitty Bennet. He thought of targeting the youngest sister but realized that Miss Kitty followed her younger sister into all her chosen activities. As a result, the second youngest would be more likely to follow his lead as well.

When Miss Lydia was involved in a game of cards, Wickham took a seat next to Miss Kitty. "How lovely you look this evening, Miss Catherine."

Kitty looked at the gentleman in surprise. It was rare that a gentleman singled her out. Usually, the only gentlemen who paid attention to Kitty were the ones whom Lydia ignored, and Kitty knew the only reason they paid attention to her was to stay near her younger sister.

"Good evening, Mr. Wickham. How did you enjoy your first day with the militia?"

"The duties were not difficult and my companions seem to be pleasant fellows."

"What brought you to the militia, sir?"

*Could things be any more perfect?* wondered Wickham. "Actually, it was not my first choice for a profession, but it became a necessity."

"What do you mean?"

"I grew up on a large estate in Derbyshire. The owner, Mr. Darcy, was my godfather."

"But Mr. Darcy is too young to be your godfather," said Kitty in confusion.

"Unfortunately, my godfather passed away some years ago, but he does have a son."

"Then it must be the son we met. He seems to be a very nice man and he is friends with Mr. Bingley, who is also very pleasant," was Kitty's artless reply.

"I guess Darcy can be polite if he chooses, but he has always hated me. My godfather, Mr. Darcy's father, and I were very close. Once he told me he wished I were his son and not Fitzwilliam." Kitty did not say anything, so Wickham continued. "The elder Mr. Darcy promised he would take care of me. In his will, he left me a living in the church that was his to give."

"Then why are you in the militia?"

"The younger Mr. Darcy chose to deny me the gift, leaving me penniless and forced to find a means of supporting myself."

"Well, I think you are much more handsome in a red coat than you would be if you dressed like Mr. Collins," replied Kitty. "You will find the militia much more fun, as there are always parties and balls to which soldiers are invited." This was not the response for which Wickham was hoping. The young lady did not seem at all sympathetic to his plight.

"Remaining near my home, attending to a peaceful calling like the church and caring for my parishioners, would have suited me quite well," sighed Wickham wistfully.

"Well, I for one am glad things worked out the way they did or you would never have come to Meryton."

Wickham sighed in frustration and excused himself. Perhaps he should speak to Miss Lydia after all, but how to do it without letting Miss Kitty see him? He would not wish to anger the sisters and turn them both against him, for this would defeat his purposes. Perhaps Miss Bennet would be a better choice, unless Darcy told his friend about their history. No, it would have to be Miss Lydia. She was a flirt. With enough flattery, he should be able to bend the young girl to his will.

As the evening ended, Mr. Wickham maneuvered Kitty into line ahead of Mary and Mr. Collins before saying his goodnights. He stepped back as she exited. When Mr. Collins began his long-winded speech expressing his thanks,

Wickham approached Lydia, who was behind the rest of her family, waiting for her chance to say her farewells.

"I am sorry we did not have much of an opportunity to speak this evening. You are quite the loveliest young lady I have seen in a very long time. I should like to get to know you better." Wickham flashed a charming smile at the young lady, who fluttered her lashes at the handsome soldier in his bright red jacket.

"We are often in Meryton. Perhaps we shall meet again soon." The others in Lydia's party were exiting her aunt's front door. Lydia gave a sashaying little walk, swaying her hips, as she moved away from Mr. Wickham. This time, his smile was more calculating than charming, but the youngest Bennet sister did not notice.

# THE TRUTH COMES OUT

On Friday, Elizabeth took breakfast in her room. At eleven that morning, when visitors arrived, she appeared in the sitting room without her disguise. Mr. Collins' eyes bulged at the sight of her from his seat beside Mary. However, due to the visitors, he was unable to question her unexpected change of appearance. Lieutenants Denny and Wickham and Mr. Bingley arrived to call within minutes of each other. Elizabeth anxiously anticipated Darcy's return. It surprised her how much she missed his presence in her daily life. While she was distracted with thoughts of William, Wickham positioned himself on a settee next to Elizabeth.

"It is a pleasure to meet you, Miss Elizabeth. I am sorry you did not accompany your sisters into Meryton on the day we met. It seems they left the true gem of the family behind."

Elizabeth's tinkling laugh met his statement. It was apparent to her that Mr. Wickham was a practiced flatterer, so rather than respond, she asked, "How do you like life in the militia?"

Mr. Wickham allowed sadness to briefly cross his face before he gave Elizabeth a tight, bright smile. "Though it was not my first choice for a profession, the experience is not unpleasant."

"If you did not wish to be a soldier, why did you join the militia?"

139

"I was to be a clergyman, but the living that was promised to me by my godfather was denied to me by his son."

A warning resounded in Elizabeth's head. The story sounded familiar, but she could not immediately recall why. However, Elizabeth did not wish to hear more of his tale of woe. "That is unfortunate. It is good that you can move beyond your misfortunes."

"With no other choice before me, moving forward was the only option. The young Mr. Darcy saw to it that my life would be as difficult as he could make it."

Elizabeth stiffened at Darcy's name. Could this be the man about whom Darcy told her? Perhaps, with subtle questioning, she could learn what story he was spreading about William.

"Are you speaking of Mr. Fitzwilliam Darcy of Derbyshire?"

"Indeed, I am. Do you know the man?"

"We met at an assembly shortly after he arrived in Meryton. It was obvious that he was unhappy to be present at such a countrified event."

"That sounds like the proud and disdainful Darcy I know." Wickham went on to tell the same story that William had told her, though he conveniently left out the part about having received payment for the living he refused.

"How shocking!" said Elizabeth. As she finished speaking, the mantle clock chimed. Looking at the time, Elizabeth said, "Please excuse me, Mr. Wickham. I must take some tea to my father."

Elizabeth moved to the tea tray. Wickham smirked as he watched her walk away.

Upon setting a cup of tea in front of her father, Elizabeth spoke to him. "Papa, I need you to join us in the sitting room. There is a visitor here who is telling lies about William." Elizabeth related to her father the things she had learned from William early in their relationship, though she did not name his sister as the young woman whom Wickham had targeted. "William should be arriving soon and I do not know how Mr. Wickham will act should he be confronted by his misdeeds. Even if you are not needed to keep order, you will find Mr. Wickham amusing. He seems to think he is irresistible to women. I doubt that Lydia or Kitty are mature enough to recognize his practiced charm, but I found him rather transparent."

Elizabeth and Mr. Bennet reached the foyer just as Mrs. Hill opened the door to Mr. Darcy and an unknown gentleman.

"Welcome back, Mr. Darcy. I missed you." Elizabeth greeted William with a brilliant smile.

"I am delighted to be back, Miss Elizabeth," said Darcy as he bowed over her hand and brought it to his lips for a kiss. "Allow me to introduce you to my cousin, Colonel Richard Fitzwilliam. He had a few days' leave and wished to join me for a rest in the country. Richard, this is Mr. Thomas Bennet and his second daughter, Miss Elizabeth."

Richard bowed in acknowledgment of the introductions. "It is a pleasure to meet you both. I have heard much about you—particularly you, Miss Elizabeth."

"Are you ready to announce your courtship, Mr. Darcy?"

"Indeed, I am, Mr. Bennet. This week has been very long waiting to hear that announcement."

"Mr. Darcy, before we enter, I should warn you of something."

A worried expression appeared on Darcy's face. "Is something amiss, Miss Elizabeth?"

"Not with us," was her encouraging reply. "However, you will find an unpleasant visitor when we enter the sitting room. Apparently, Mr. George Wickham recently joined the militia stationed here in Meryton. I believe my sisters met him on Tuesday."

At the mention of Wickham's name, both gentlemen's expressions became exceedingly grim. Then the colonel's slowly changed to a smug grin. "I believe that Wickham has effectively hanged himself this time, Darcy."

"What do you mean?"

"Militiamen are subject to following orders from any superior officer. Are the papers showing Wickham's debts with you, or would you need to send for them?"

"I always carry them in case I should ever encounter him. They are in my trunk."

"Ask your valet to locate them. We will finally have Wickham where we want him and, more importantly where he deserves to be."

Darcy stepped out the door and gave instructions to his Evans.

"Mr. Bennet, does the magistrate live nearby?"

"Yes, he is my neighbor, Sir William Lucas."

"How long would it take this Lucas to arrive? Would you please direct a servant to retrieve him as soon as possible?"

"It should take only about twenty minutes." Mr. Bennet turned to Mrs. Hill, who had remained in the hall, waiting for instruction. "Please send Sam from the stables to Lucas Lodge. Let Sir William know that we need him in his official capacity."

"Of course, sir." The housekeeper bobbed a curtsey and turned towards the back of the house. The group was distracted from watching the housekeeper by the entrance of Darcy's valet through the front door.

"Here are the papers you wanted, sir."

Darcy took the sheaf of papers the servant handed him.

"Now that everything is in place, I believe it is time to greet our old friend," said Richard with a grin. "After you, Mr. Bennet."

Expecting to enjoy the events about to play out, Mr. Bennet opened the door to the sitting room. "Look who has returned and come to visit us so soon upon his arrival," said Mr. Bennet as he entered the room. He was followed by Elizabeth on Mr. Darcy's arm. The colonel brought up the rear.

Mrs. Bennet looked up and cried, "Mr. Darcy, how nice of you to visit. And who is this with you?" Both Mrs. Bennet and her two youngest daughters were eyeing the colonel speculatively.

"This is my cousin, Colonel Richard Fitzwilliam, of the regulars."

"Welcome to Longbourn, Colonel Fitzwilliam. Please be seated, gentlemen."

When Wickham saw who had entered the room, he moved to stand with his back to the others. He looked out the window, hoping to avoid discovery. As soon as conversation distracted the others, Wickham would sneak from the room.

Upon hearing footsteps enter the room, Wickham edged along the wall, hoping to make it to the hall without detection.

Unfortunately, before he had gone more than a few steps, Wickham felt a firm grip on his shoulder. "Well, well, well, whom do we have here?"

Wickham's stomach dropped as he heard the voice of the only man whom he feared. Plastering a pleasant smile on his face, Wickham turned in the only way possible, bringing the colonel's arm to rest along his shoulders as he faced his antagonist. "Why, Fitzwilliam, fancy meeting you here."

"Up to your old tricks, again, Wickham, and still telling the same tired tales."

"I am sure I do not know what you mean."

"Come now, Wickham. Do not be coy. How many people have heard your misleading tale of suffering at Darcy's hand?"

Wickham did not say anything.

"You mean you did not tell anyone that Darcy denied you a living and forced you to seek other employment?"

Kitty spoke up. "He told me that tale the night after we met. I told him he was lucky not to wear the black of a parson because he looks much better in a red coat."

Richard smiled at Kitty's naiveté. "Did he perhaps mention that he had refused the living and received a total of four thousand pounds for it, which he gambled away within a year?"

All of the females in the room gasped in shock.

"He wasted four thousand pounds in one year?" asked Mrs. Bennet.

"Indeed, he did, madam. Georgie here is a wastrel, gambler, and drunkard, among other things. One of his favorite tricks is to run up debts and then slip away without paying them." Fitzwilliam turned to the man still firmly in his grip. "How much debt did you manage to accumulate in your few days in Meryton, Georgie?"

"Now, Fitzwilliam, why would you want to tell these fine people such ridiculous stories? I am sure you are not trying to ruin my reputation with these excellent folk." There was an undertone of menace in Wickham's voice as he spoke. His eyes wore a hard expression.

"Now, Georgie, how can I be ruining your reputation by telling the truth? Darcy carries the documents you signed when you relinquished the living. He also purchased all of your debts in Lambton, Cambridge, and any others that merchants presented to him for payment. Unfortunately for you, you made a fatal mistake this time."

"Again, your disturbing sense of humor rears its head, Fitzwilliam. What mistake have I supposedly made?"

"Darcy carries with him the papers regarding your debts, in the event that you again crossed his path. As such, I will be accompanying you to Marshalsea. With debts as high as yours, you may never see the light of day again." Richard could not restrain a little chuckle.

The blood rushed from Wickham's face, leaving him quite pale. Lowering his voice, he spoke through gritted teeth, "I will destroy Georgiana if you do not let me walk out of this room."

"I cannot allow you to do that. As a member of the militia, you are subject to the authority of any superior officer. Since I outrank you, you are subject to me." The two men glared at each other.

Not wanting to give Wickham time to speak, Darcy leaned over to Mr. Bennet. "I believe now would be the perfect time to make our announcement," Darcy whispered.

Mr. Bennet looked surprised but acquiesced at younger man's encouraging nod. The focus of all those in the room had been on the conversation between the two military men. "Your attention, please." Several started at the sound of Mr. Bennet's voice. "I would like to announce the courtship of my daughter, Elizabeth, to Mr. Fitzwilliam Darcy."

Mr. Collins, who had been unable to take his eyes from Elizabeth since her first appearance in the room, cried, "Mr. Darcy cannot be courting Cousin Elizabeth, as he is engaged to his cousin, Miss de Bourgh!"

"Be quiet, Mr. Collins. We are dealing with the matter of Lieutenant Wickham. Anything else will have to wait."

At Mr. Bennet's pronouncement, Wickham's mouth fell open in shock. Darcy engaged to a mere country miss? It was beyond belief. However, to distract everyone's attention away from himself, Wickham was quick to second Mr. Collins' pronouncement. "Mr. Collins speaks the truth! Lady Catherine de Bourgh has spoken of the engagement forever. She claims it was the wish of Darcy's mother and herself that their children be engaged upon Anne's birth."

"Quiet, Wickham," said Richard. "Attempting to stir the pot will not change your situation."

Wickham thought frantically, searching for something else he could use to gain his freedom. He said the first thing that came into his head. "I am surprised, Mr. Bennet, that you would allow your daughter to court a man whose sister is ruined. It will disgrace all of your daughters by association."

"If you are referring to your failed attempt to run away with a fifteen-year-old child so that you could control her large dowry, I am already aware of that. I also know that Mr. Darcy thwarted your attempt. Consequently, I see no reason to prevent the relationship."

"I swear to you, Darcy, you let me go or I will ruin your sister. When I am through with her, she will never be able to show her face in town again," ground out Wickham.

Darcy tensed at Wickham's words and took a step forward. He paused, however, when Elizabeth placed her hand on his arm. A look passed between the couple and Darcy relaxed somewhat.

"Mr. Wickham, when those to whom you told your ridiculous stories learn they were all lies, why would they believe anything else you might say, particularly if you managed to run up any debts during your short visit? Nor will anyone present say anything which could damage the reputation of a sweet young girl who might someday be a part of our family." Darcy smiled so widely at Elizabeth's words, his dimples appeared.

Richard grinned at Wickham and said, "What makes you think you will be speaking to anyone before you are placed in your cell at Marshalsea?"

Again Wickham's face paled. "You cannot simply lock me up like that." His voice did not sound as confident as he wished.

"Actually, I can. The one and only person you will see is the jailor. Moreover, you can be sure he will know of your so-called charm. Nothing there comes without a price—not food, not paper, not a blanket for warmth—and you will have nothing with which to buy yourself any comforts. Your debts will see you locked up until you are old and gray— if you live that long," added Richard carelessly.

Wickham attempted to wrestle his shoulder from Richard's grip, which was so tight as to cause a feeling of numbness in his arm. Wickham gazed around the room, looking for a sign of sympathy. Every eye he met was cold. They glared at him the same way a housekeeper looked at a puddle of mud on a clean carpet. He would get no help from any of the Bennets.

At just that moment, the sitting-room door opened. Everyone turned to look. Mrs. Hill appeared in the opening to announce, "Sir William Lucas to see you, sir."

With everyone distracted, Wickham twisted with all his might. He managed to break the hold the colonel had on him and dashed for the window, planning to leap out and escape. However, Wickham did not count on Lydia Bennet, who shoved a chair in his path mid-leap. He hit the chair, knocking it over backward. His back leg caught on the upturned chair and Wickham flew head-first into the wall, knocking himself unconscious.

When he came to, his hands and feet were bound. Lydia Bennet was leaning over him. "A scoundrel like you does not deserve to escape. Seeing you tied up is far more fitting! You tried to mislead my sisters, lied about a gentleman who likes my sister, and tried to hurt a young girl. You deserve whatever it is that happens to you. I must thank you, however, Mr. Wickham, for opening my eyes to how untrustworthy some gentlemen can be." Lydia gave the gentleman a kick for good measure as she strode away.

Wickham's humiliation was complete. Most of those in the room were laughing at him as he lay there trussed up like a pig, his nose broken by the feel of it.

"I will happily sign the papers that will commit this scoundrel to Marshalsea," said Sir William. "Perhaps we could ask Mr. Philips to attend us to help with the legalities."

Mr. Bennet turned to the housekeeper. Before he spoke, Mrs. Hill bashfully said, "I sent a boy for him at the same time I sent someone for Sir William, sir. I hope that is acceptable."

"Of course, Mrs. Hill. I congratulate you on your forethought." The housekeeper looked relieved at his words.

At that moment, there was a knock at the door. Mrs. Hill opened it and admitted Mr. Phillips.

The gentlemen adjourned to Mr. Bennet's study, leaving the trussed-up Wickham on the sitting room floor. It did not take them long to prepare the necessary papers. When the group rejoined the ladies, they noticed a gag tied around Wickham's face.

When Lydia observed the gentlemen's grins, she explained. "First he was trying to convince us that we should release him. When that didn't work, he started abusing us. I got tired of listening to him."

The explanation evoked a bigger laugh from all of the gentlemen. A muffled invective sounded from the general direction of the bound officer.

When this contretemps had begun, Lieutenant Denny, who was also visiting with Wickham and the Bennets, made his excuses and departed. Seeing that a higher ranking officer was attempting to take away Wickham, he went to retrieve Colonel Forster.

Just as Richard was about to ask for assistance in taking Wickham back to camp before transporting him to London, Mrs. Hill appeared in the doorway to the sitting room. "Colonel Forster and Lieutenant Denny."

"I understand someone is attempting to remove Mr. Wickham from my unit," began the new arrival loudly.

"Why, Forster, you old dog! What are you doing in Meryton?"

Colonel Forster turned in the direction of the familiar voice. "Is that you, Fitzwilliam? What brings you here?"

"I came to visit my cousin Mr. Darcy and his friend Bingley for a day or two. However, to my surprise, I found a scoundrel in the midst of a room full of ladies."

"Do you refer to Wickham?"

"I do. We just completed the papers to deliver the scoundrel to Marshalsea."

"If you are taking him there, he must be a debtor."

Richard nodded.

"Indeed," announced Mr. Philips, "to the tune of over six thousand pounds." The ladies in the room gasped at the amount.

"He is also a drunkard, gambler, cheater, liar, and debaucher," Richard informed them.

Colonel Forster's eyes widened at each word. "Well, then, I believe it would be appropriate to strip him of his rank and retain the funds he paid for it."

Wickham's feet kicked the floor for attention. Again a muffled sound came from his corner of the room. His commanding officer gave him a withering look. "You obviously did not read the contract you signed, and I quote, "Disgraced officers can be stripped of their rank and lose the cost of their commission for actions unbecoming to an officer.""

"Forster, might you spare a few men who could help me escort this rogue to the jail in London?"

"Certainly, Fitzwilliam. I will send three of my largest and strongest men with you. We would not want this disgrace of a man to escape. It is getting late in the day. I will lock him in the brig, on bread and water, until the day of your departure. Enjoy your planned visit. We will keep this scoundrel under control."

Within a short time, Wickham was thrown over a horse and being led back to the militia encampment. Sir William and Mr. Philips departed, and Mrs. Bennet invited the gentlemen to stay and dine. Once the gentlemen accepted, Mr. Collins stood, saying, "Mr. Bennet, I must protest."

# MR. COLLINS MAKES A FUSS

"What is it that you must protest?"

"As I stated earlier, Mr. Darcy cannot be courting Cousin Elizabeth. His engagement to his cousin, Miss de Bourgh, took place at her birth twenty-five years ago. Not only that, but Cousin Elizabeth lied by disguising her beauty in the time since my arrival to force my choice towards another. As she is the second in both age and beauty, I demand that I be granted her hand in marriage."

"You blundering fool," Darcy said. "You grossly insulted the lovely and kind Miss Mary. You, sir, are no gentleman. Nor can Mr. Bennet grant you Miss Elizabeth's hand in marriage, as he agreed to our courtship a week ago. I shall never relinquish it."

"But Miss de Bourgh–" whined Collins.

Darcy interrupted the man. "I am not engaged to my cousin. It was my aunt who wished this, but neither of my parents agreed. Unlike my aunt, my parents made a love match, and they desired the same for me, not some arranged affair devoid of feeling."

"But how can you not care for Miss de Bourgh? She is one of the most beautiful flowers in all of England," declared Mr. Collins.

"I do care for Anne, but not in a way that makes me desire marriage to her. I am not bound to marry my cousin, either legally or by inclination. I am free to choose my future, and it does not include Miss de Bourgh as my wife."

Darcy glared at Collins as he spoke while giving Elizabeth's hand a reassuring squeeze. He was very relieved to feel her answering squeeze.

"But someone as grand and important as Lady Catherine cannot be incorrect. Do you mean to tell me that you will disappoint your family and not fulfill your duty to your cousin? If you are concerned about Miss Elizabeth, you need not be; I will willingly marry her in your place."

"You presume a great deal, Mr. Collins," said Elizabeth in harsh tones. "I hardly know you, and from what I have learned, I know that we are most unsuited to be marriage partners. Not to mention, I would never accept someone who first paid court to my sister. I would never inflict such a hurt on one of my dear sisters. The fact that you would discuss this topic so blatantly in front of Mary after paying court to her for the last week only goes to prove that your feelings of affection are not real but done at the direction of your patroness."

"Hush, Lizzy," hissed Mrs. Bennet, "or Mr. Collins will not marry any of you."

"You forget yourself, Mrs. Bennet, and you as well, Mr. Collins," said Mr. Bennet. "It is I who must approve any marriage, and no one has sought my permission for such an event."

"Why should you not grant me your permission to marry any of my dear cousins?" demanded Mr. Collins.

"Why? Because I desire that my girls are all settled with someone who will love and care for them—and that entails much more than just a roof over their heads and an interfering patroness."

"For someone who has not yet met her, you certainly understand Lady Catherine," laughed Richard.

"You would insult your aunt in such a way," cried the shocked parson.

"Mr. Collins, it seems that you confuse my aunt with the Almighty. As a minister of the church, is it not the Lord to whom you owe your allegiance and efforts rather than to Lady Catherine?"

"With Lady Catherine's nobility and wisdom, I am sure the Lord is in agreement with all of her suggestions." With this pronouncement, everyone in the room burst into laughter, upon which Mr. Collins looked highly indignant.

"Let me make myself perfectly clear, sir," said Darcy as he stared at the parson. "My affairs are of no concern to my aunt, and she has no right to any information about my situation with Miss Elizabeth. Should you say anything to her about my courtship or anything else related to myself and Miss Elizabeth, either verbally or in writing, I will be obliged to call you out. Nor will you speak about Miss Elizabeth in any way. Do I make myself clear?"

Mr. Collins' eyes grew rounder at Darcy's threats. "But I owe my great good fortune to my esteemed patroness. She is nearly your closest relative, Mr. Darcy. Of course she is entitled to know all of your affairs."

"Mr. Collins," said the colonel as he gently stroked the handle of his sword. "I believe you should heed my cousin's words. For if you do not and you somehow survive your encounter with him, I shall be forced to challenge you, and I can promise that you will not walk away from that."

"Now, now, Richard. I doubt we will need to resort to violence. I am sure Mr. Collins understands the situation. not wish your father's friend, the Bishop of London, to learn that he puts the wishes of his patroness above those of his parish and church duties. I wonder what might happen should such a thing occur. Do you think the bishop might have Mr. Collins reassigned? Or perhaps he could even lose his parish?"

Mr. Collins was torn. He dared not disappoint his patroness, but neither did he wish to find himself in a parish that would endanger his life. Collins would ponder the situation overnight. Perhaps he might woo Cousin Elizabeth away from Lady Catherine's nephew, thereby resolving the issue. For the remainder of the evening, he stayed away from Mary while studying Elizabeth and Mr. Darcy. His observations did not reassure. There was as obvious a connection between them as he had witnessed between Cousin Jane and Mr. Bingley. Then a devious thought made its way into his head...but could he do it? What if he arranged a compromise of Cousin Elizabeth? But would that make him a target of Mr. Darcy's anger? The thought that occurred next caused him to gasp aloud. Fortunately, no one was paying attention to him. *If I can get her away from the house, perhaps I can elope with her to Gretna Green. Mr. Darcy could do nothing if we were married when he discovered us or when we returned. It would also increase my worth in Lady Catherine's eyes, as it would force Mr. Darcy to oblige his aunt and marry Miss de Bourgh.* An odd smile settled on Mr. Collins' features and he continued his quiet observance until retiring for the night.

The next morning, Bingley, Darcy, and Richard broke their fast early before the ladies came down. Then they settled in the library as they awaited an appropriate time to visit the Bennets.

"Darcy, I know the lovely Miss Elizabeth occupied all your attention last evening, but I fear there may be a problem."

"What do you mean, Richard?"

"I kept an eye on Collins as discreetly as possible. He is obviously unwilling to risk being challenged, but he emitted a gasp. When I looked, his eyes were wide and I could almost see the wheels turning in his mind. At some point, I believe he came up with a scheme to get what he wants and make Lady Catherine happy as well. We will need to keep a close eye on him—and more particularly on Miss Elizabeth. It may be wise to alert Mr. Bennet of a possible problem."

Before Darcy could reply, the sound of Miss Bingley's strident voice reached them.

Bingley looked at Darcy. "Are we ready to announce our courtships to my family?"

"Do you not think we can wait until we are announcing engagements?" Darcy asked. "That will allow us a great deal more peace. I do not wish to contend with your sister's possibly desperate attention, which I can only imagine will increase, for any longer than necessary."

"Perhaps I can convince Hurst to return the ladies to town for the little season. That would allow us to enjoy our courtships without interruption or distractions."

Richard laughed. "Do you really think your sister will leave with Darcy in residence?"

"Perhaps you will need to make a quick trip somewhere and not know when you will return, even if you plan to return the next day," chuckled Bingley. The other gentlemen joined in the laughter.

"Do you think we will be able to spend the time we wish to with the Bennets without Caroline's knowledge of the connection?" wondered Darcy.

"Undoubtedly, Caroline will complain about the time we are spending away from the estate, but we can always set out to examine some portion of the estate and then visit the Bennets without her knowledge." Bingley's grin was irrepressible. Soon, two more smiles appeared.

Glancing at his pocket watch, Darcy said, "It seems we managed to avoid the ladies this morning. It is now an appropriate time to visit."

"What shall be our destination today, at least as far as Caroline is concerned?" asked Bingley.

"I think you need to show me your estate," suggested Richard. "That should take us quite a bit of time."

Bingley pulled the bell cord and a footman soon knocked on the door. "Please have our horses saddled. We will be out momentarily."

The footman nodded and left to pass on the master's instructions.

"Let us greet the family and make our excuses, shall we?" Again, Bingley's infectious grin appeared.

Caroline heard the laughter coming towards the dining room and wondered what would possibly cause such joviality so early in the morning. She was not fond of the morning and would much prefer to remain in her room until time for luncheon. However, with Mr. Darcy in residence, she could not afford to be unavailable for so much of the day. Consequently, she pasted a smile on her face and attempted to meet the gentlemen with an equally pleasant appearance.

By the time they reached the door, Mr. Darcy was wearing his usual solemn expression. "Good morning," said Bingley. "We have already broken our fast and are planning to tour the estate."

"Please do not keep our guests out too long, Charles. It seems Mr. Darcy is never here. I thought the whole point of his visit was to relax and enjoy time with his closest friends."

"No, Miss Bingley, that was not the point of my visit. It was to help your brother learn to manage an estate. If we are often absent during the day, then I am accomplishing my purpose. There is still much to do, and I may be required to depart soon. I do not know when I might be able to return."

"When must you leave?"

"I am not certain when or if I will need to leave, though it is possible I will be away much of the time, even if I remain in the area. I may need to make several trips to London. You might find your time better spent enjoying the little season."

Caroline thought for a moment. "Perhaps you are right, Mr. Darcy. If you will always be out on the estate with Charles, perhaps we would see more of each other if I were also in London. I do so enjoy the many events that take place during the little season."

"I would not take my plans into consideration when making yours. If I am in

London, I will be attending to business. When I can return to Netherfield Park, we will be out on the estate or sequestered with the steward, for there is still a great deal for Charles to learn. I would recommend that you enjoy the little season. You might even find someone who enjoys society as much as you do."

Surprised by his words, Caroline did not know what to say in response. Staring, she could read nothing in his expression. However, as she was not easily discouraged, she said with a laugh, "As a member of the first circles, you must enjoy society as much as I, Mr. Darcy."

"Indeed not," replied the gentleman with more warmth in his tone than that to which she was accustomed. "I would happily spend all my time at Pemberley were it not for the need to maintain contacts until Georgiana makes her debut. If I were to find the proper wife, we might visit town to shop or attend the theater on occasion, for she would also prefer the country as much as I do."

"You would prefer to spend all of your time at Pemberley?" asked a shocked Caroline.

'Yes, I would. I would not spend more than a month in town if I could help it."

"But, of course, you would give first consideration to your wife's preferences, would you not?"

"I would have considered such things before marrying, Miss Bingley, and would hope that my wife and I wanted the same things in our life together."

Before Caroline could say more, Bingley said, "The horses are ready. We should not keep them standing." With that, the three gentlemen bowed and departed.

"Well done, Darcy," said the colonel as the trio started down the driveway. "I think that you did her a great favor by being honest with her."

"I think you shocked Caroline," said Bingley with a laugh. "I have never seen her look at you in such a way. It will be interesting to discover how she reacts to you after what you said."

"If my words make a difference, I shall be quite surprised. I shall also need to consider being more forthright with others who impose themselves on me."

When the gentlemen were halfway to Longbourn, Richard said, "Darcy, I think you should allow me to speak to Mr. Bennet about my observations. You should discuss with Miss Elizabeth, and perhaps all of her sisters, the necessity of keeping an eye on her and not ever allowing her to be alone with Mr. Collins."

"That is a good suggestion. Unfortunately, I do not know how we can get the ladies alone without Mr. Collins intruding, especially if you are correct about his intentions."

"Why do we not walk with our ladies and then allow them to discuss the matter with their sisters?"

"Excellent idea, Bingley. I will try to see Mr. Bennet as soon as we arrive. When I return to the parlor, I will keep Collins occupied so that you may walk."

The gentlemen arrived shortly thereafter. When they entered, the colonel asked to be shown to Mr. Bennet before announcing the others. Everything was quickly arranged to the gentlemen's satisfaction, and Richard entered Mr. Bennet's study.

"Good morning, Colonel Fitzwilliam. What can I do for you this morning?"

"Mr. Bennet, after Mr. Collins' behavior last evening, I kept an eye on him. After you departed from the company, something occurred which leads me to believe we might have a problem."

"What do you mean, Colonel?"

Richard went on to tell the older man what he had observed and what his suspicions were.

When he finished speaking, Mr. Bennet's expression was thoughtful. After several moments, he spoke. "My cousin Collins, the current gentleman's father, was an uneducated brute. I would guess from my cousin's strange mix of subservience and pride that he might have a suppressed mean streak. It would not be surprising based on who raised him."

"I have already spoken with Darcy and Bingley regarding the matter," Richard said. "As well as alerting you to the situation, they plan to speak to Miss Bennet and Miss Elizabeth. They are waiting for me to join them before asking the ladies to walk. I will engage Mr. Collins to be sure he cannot follow them. They plan to ask the ladies to inform their sisters of the situation. Our goal is to ensure that Miss Elizabeth is never alone, thereby giving Mr. Collins no chance to enact a compromise of any kind."

"You must be a brilliant tactician, Colonel, for your plan is excellent. Are you as good with a game of chess?"

"I enjoy the game and often play with Darcy."

"Perhaps you might join me for a game sometime during your visit?"

"I would enjoy that, sir. Now, I should join the others so that I might distract Mr. Collins and allow the others to discuss our plan."

"Would you like me to join you briefly in the distraction effort?"

"You are welcome to do so, sir, if you wish, but I am sure I can handle the gentleman."

"I am sure you can, and I believe I will accompany you because it will be enjoyable to witness you in action, Colonel."

In a spirit of fellowship, the gentlemen departed from Mr. Bennet's study and joined the others in the sitting room. Mr. Collins' back was to the doorway, so he missed the exchange between the colonel and his cousin. Mr. Darcy was also impressed that Mr. Bennet joined the group; it meant he took Richard's warning seriously.

Knowing just the approach to take with a man of Mr. Collins' temperament, Richard said, "Good morning, Mr. Collins. How are you today?"

The parson turned at the sound of the new voice, pleased at receiving the attention of the Earl of Matlock's son. Standing, he bowed to the officer. "I am well, thank you, Colonel Fitzwilliam. I hope you are well."

"Indeed, I am enjoying my sojourn in the country."

"Did you just arrive?"

"No, I happened upon the colonel as the gentleman arrived," said Mr. Bennet. "With my love of military history and strategy, I induced him to join me in conversation."

"We also discovered a mutual enjoyment of the game of chess. I hope to join Mr. Bennet in a game or two during my visit."

The gentlemen settled in chairs near Mr. Collins, engaging him in conversation and flattering his rather large ego. About ten minutes later, Mr. Bennet excused himself from the room with a reminder to the colonel to join him in a game of chess on his next visit. With Mr. Bennet's departure, the colonel moved to sit closer to the ladies and direct some of his attention to them.

At the defection of the gentlemen, Mr. Collins returned his attention to his observations of Mr. Darcy and Miss Elizabeth. He was shocked, however, to discover that they were no longer present in the room. Mr. Collins looked all around, even moving into the small alcove where the piano stood. At that point, he realized that the tall windows in the room opened onto the terrace. Mr. Collins looked out those same windows but could see no one.

Turning to the room, he said, "Where has Miss Elizabeth gone?"

Colonel Fitzwilliam stared at the man, but it was Mrs. Bennet who answered. "I assume they went for a walk, as they often do. Lizzy loves to walk, and Mr. Darcy seems to enjoy it as well." She then turned back to her conversation with her younger daughters.

Mr. Collins maintained his post at the window, waiting for the others to return. However, as he stood there, a new idea came into his mind. *If I can rise early enough to depart before Cousin Elizabeth, I might be able to follow her and manage my compromise of the little tart. One thing is certain: I will enjoy breaking her of these ridiculous behaviors once she is my wife.*

The colonel continued his covert observation of the parson and did not like what he saw. He would have to suggest to Mr. Bennet that Miss Elizabeth walk with a companion in the future. Richard knew when the couples were returning, for Mr. Collins gave up his post at the window and moved to greet them when they entered the room.

They had barely stepped inside before Mr. Collins said, "I wish you had invited me to join you. It is such a lovely day." No one said anything in response, so Mr. Collins continued. "I was immediately aware of your departure, as the room seemed dim without your brilliance, Cousin Elizabeth." Elizabeth looked uncomfortable with his words. Behind the parson, Richard rolled his eyes.

"Should I be offended, Mr. Collins?" asked Richard. "I thought you were enjoying our conversation."

"I am offended, Mr. Collins," Darcy said. "It is extremely inappropriate for you to be making such comments to the lady I am courting. If you continue to make such remarks, I shall be forced to call you out."

Though nervous at having offended his patroness' nephew, Mr. Collins was determined to not back down. "No offense was intended, Mr. Darcy, and I do not see how it could be inappropriate for me to compliment any of my fair cousins."

Mrs. Bennet invited the gentlemen to remain and dine with the family. Throughout the afternoon, Mr. Collins sat separate from most of the family, but near to Elizabeth and Darcy without being too close. However, it was apparent that he was eavesdropping on their conversation, for he attempted to interject himself into their discussion on occasion. Often, he tried to draw Elizabeth into conversation with him.

Richard recognized when William was on the verge of losing his temper at the parson. At that point, Richard called to the gentleman, "Mr. Collins, I would like to ask you some questions about Rosings. Would you please join me?"

A brief look of frustration crossed the gentleman's face, but he acquiesced with as much grace as he could. Collins seated himself where he could observe the couple, biding his time until he could attempt to separate Cousin Elizabeth from the others. He was to be frustrated in his desires, however, for as soon as the gentlemen left, the Bennet sisters excused themselves from the company and disappeared into one of their bedrooms.

When Collins attempted to follow them up the stairs, Mr. Bennet requested his presence in his study. "I believe we should discuss what you know of estate management since you will one day inherit Longbourn." Mr. Bennet asked his cousin endless questions and offered him several books to read so that he could be a success when he owned the estate.

Meanwhile, the Bennet sisters gathered in Jane's room. "What is so important that we must be huddled here in this room where there are not enough comfortable seats?" whined Lydia.

"Lizzy needs our help," said Jane, her voice much more severe than any of her sisters had heard it before.

Kitty and Lydia looked at Jane in surprise. Mary asked, "What is it, Jane, Lizzy? What is the matter?"

# THWARTING MR. COLLINS

JANE, AS ELDEST, ACTED AS THE spokesperson. She explained what Colonel Fitzwilliam had witnessed and his suspicions. "We must work out a plan to keep Lizzy safe. We cannot allow Mr. Collins any chance to be alone with her or compromise her. Papa refused his permission for him to marry any of us. If he maintains that opinion, even if a compromise occurs, we would all be considered unmarriageable if word were to get out."

"Why do you say that?" questioned Lydia.

"One of the reasons Lizzy and I are always trying to rein in your exuberance a little is that if one of us has her reputation ruined, we would all share in her ruin. There is nothing wrong with your joy for life, but you must temper that and always be on your best behavior. The way you flirt with all the officers might give them the impression that you are not a proper young lady. Not only do you put yourself at risk, but you also put the reputations of your four sisters at risk."

Lydia and Kitty looked at Jane, their eyes large and their expressions confused.

However, it was Mary who spoke. "What must we do to keep Elizabeth protected from Mr. Collins?"

"Remain alert. If Lizzy wishes to walk in the morning, one of us will need to accompany her. If she and Mr. Collins are both in the same room, one of us should remain with them at all times.

Whenever she goes upstairs, or anywhere, one of us should walk with her."

"It is surprising that a clergyman would consider such an action. However, based on the inappropriate behavior Mr. Collins exhibited to date, I guess it is to be expected," Mary said.

"Is he not afraid of what Mr. Darcy or the colonel might do to him?" asked Kitty.

"The colonel's supposition is that our cousin believes that once the damage is done, it will be too late and the gentleman will not bother him."

"Is he really that big of an idiot?" wondered a surprised Lydia.

"Lydia," said Jane in a disapproving tone, though her youngest sister did not look at all abashed.

"I believe we have witnessed plenty of evidence of that since his arrival," muttered Elizabeth. All of her sisters laughed.

They continued their discussion, trying to think of every situation in which Lizzy might need protecting.

When Mr. Collins finally escaped Mr. Bennet, he went upstairs, hoping to run into Miss Elizabeth. Not trying to muffle the sound of his footsteps, he paused before a door, behind which he heard the sound of the young women's laughter. Leaning in, he placed his ear to the door.

Lydia heard his footsteps outside the door and wondered if he would attempt to eavesdrop, as she might do. Giving no thought to his reaction, she jumped up and rushed to the door, then opened it abruptly. Mr. Collins tumbled into the room at her feet.

"Did no one teach you that listening at doors was bad manners, Mr. Collins?" laughed Lydia as she stared down at the black lump on the floor.

Mr. Collins struggled to regain his feet, looking very undignified in the process. The chuckles behind him increased his anger. *Perhaps if Mr. Bennet were to die soon, I would get the opportunity to teach all of them some manners.* The thought brought a smug smile to his face. The smile remained in place as he turned to face the ladies.

"You are so droll, Cousin Lydia. I had paused to fix my shoe buckle. I thought my hand was on the wall. It was rather unladylike of you to rush from the room in such a fashion. Perhaps you should be returned to the nursery until you learn some manners."

"Only my parents may correct my manners, sir. They saw fit to release me from the nursery, so your opinion is of little import. Now, if you would please leave, my sisters and I were enjoying some time together." So saying, Lydia shut the door in the face of the stunned parson. Before the door closed all the way, the angry voice of Mr. Collins reached the sisters.

"They may control you now, and you best pray you are married before I take control, for I guarantee you will not like living under my rule." The menace in his tone was unmistakable.

Lydia turned to look at her sisters. She was not surprised to see the stunned looks on their faces, for this matched how she felt. "What do you think he meant by that?"

Jane and Elizabeth exchange a glance. This time, Elizabeth spoke. "He is angry and speaking nonsense. I am sure he wishes he had the chance to repay us for the indignities he feels we inflicted on him. In other words, his ego is bruised and he would like a chance to make us suffer, too."

"You do not think he would do anything to Papa so that he would get the chance, do you?" Kitty asked the question each of them was thinking.

"Mr. Collins seems silly and ineffectual. I hardly picture him causing physical harm to Papa," said Jane. Mary nodded her agreement.

Elizabeth spoke as Jane did to reassure her younger sisters' worries. *Could he be a threat to Papa? Is it possible, Mr. Collins would harm Papa to inherit early and control us?* Their mother would never be able to stand against him. If he controlled the girls after her father's death, Mr. Collins would prevent her relationship with Mr. Darcy and force her to marry him. Perhaps she should speak to William or her father to determine what to do.

"Since Papa already informed Mr. Collins that he might not marry any of us, why do we not just ask the gentleman to leave?" This time Mary voiced the question.

"I do not know if Papa would be willing to give up the amusement that Mr. Collins gives him," said a doubtful Elizabeth.

"Not even when your safety and the reputation of all his daughters might be in question?" Again, it was Mary who spoke.

The sisters looked at one another. "I believe we should approach Papa as a group and present our request," announced Lydia. "If he sees that we are all serious in our request, it might make him more inclined to act."

"Mr. Collins will be even angrier with all of us. Should anything happen to Father, things would be even more difficult."

"Just because he inherits Longbourn does not mean he will exert any control over us. Let us hope he is not intelligent enough to realize that."

Their decision made, the girls went en masse to visit their father in his sanctuary. Needless to say, he was startled when he called out to enter and all five of his daughters stepped into the room.

"This is an unexpected surprise. What may I do for my dear daughters?"

Jane, again, served as the voice of all. "Papa, we wish to discuss a few serious matters with you." She paused to wait for her father's permission to continue. At his nod, Jane and Elizabeth seated themselves in the chairs before his desk. The younger girls seated themselves on the sofa along the wall. When everyone was settled, Jane continued. "We learned of Colonel Fitzwilliam's concerns for Lizzy's safety. We would like to request that you ask Mr. Collins to leave. You denied him permission to marry any of us. We see no reason why he should remain where he is not wanted."

"You realize his anger would increase if I were to do so."

"We do realize that, Papa, and that leads me to our other concern. Will Mr. Collins have any control over us upon your death?"

"Why would you ask that?"

Lydia spoke up, telling her father of what had occurred when they caught him listening at the door, as well as about the muttered comment as he walked away.

"We are concerned for you, Papa," said Mary. Kitty nodded her agreement.

"Concerned for me?" Mr. Bennet's face expressed a contrast of emotions. He was surprised at the concern they showed and the intelligence of the conversation.

It was Elizabeth who answered his question. "My younger sisters are concerned that Mr. Collins might attempt to hurt you so that he would inherit. They simply want to be sure that he will not be our guardian."

"Though discussing my death is not something I care to do, if it will ease your minds, I will tell you about some of the arrangements."

"I do not think you need to tell us more than about our guardianship, Papa, if it makes you uncomfortable," said Jane.

"There is money set aside for the improvement of the dowager's cottage. You younger girls will live there with your mother. Mr. Philips will be your official guardian. Jane and Elizabeth, you will reside in London with the Gardiners, and he will be your guardian. If any of you marry before I die, the arrangements may be adjusted as needed. Mr. Collins will inherit Longbourn, but he shall have no say in your futures, nor shall he be able to turn your mother out of the dower house." He looked at each of the girls in turn to ensure they understood. "Does that ease your concerns?"

Five voices answered, "Yes, Papa."

"Now, Lizzy, are you truly concerned about Mr. Collins' presence? I will ask him to leave if you are."

Elizabeth looked at her sisters and received an unspoken answer from each. "I am not concerned for myself, but I am concerned for you. Though he will not have a say in our future, we would not wish to lose you before the Lord decides it is your time." Her sisters nodded their agreement.

"Perhaps I do not say it often enough, but I love you, Papa," said Kitty shyly.

"Me too, Papa, and I will try to behave with more propriety in the future," Lydia said. "Jane and Lizzy helped me understand how my behavior might affect my sisters."

"What do you wish me to do about Mr. Collins? Shall he be allowed to stay, or shall I send him home?"

"He can stay for the time being," said Elizabeth. "However, I would ask you to keep a close eye on him. Should you see behavior that concerns you, please ask him to leave. If we provide a reason for asking, he can have no grounds on which to complain, can he?"

"I believe that is a wise decision. However, I doubt it will prevent the man from complaining." Mr. Bennet grinned. "I must tell you how much I enjoyed this discussion. I am proud of the seriousness with which you addressed your concerns. I hope that perhaps we can all grow closer in the future."

"Papa, would you be willing to teach us the way you did Jane and Lizzy?" asked Lydia. Kitty nodded in agreement.

Mr. Bennet could not hide his surprise at the request. It would appear that his youngest daughters' exposure to the unusual situations they encountered recently had brought about a mighty change in them. It delighted him and he hoped that the change would last.

"Kitty, Lydia, and you too, Mary, if you wish, why do we not meet tomorrow? I can learn a little more about what things might interest you. You might also ask Mrs. Hill to begin instructing you about the household matters so you will be prepared to run a home of your own."

The girls stood up to depart, and Mr. Bennet rose as well. He walked to the door and opened it for the girls, kissing each on her forehead as she exited.

Closing the door after the last one departed, Mr. Bennet leaned against it with a smile on his face. How many changes the arrival of the Netherfield party and their guests had brought to Longbourn. The gentlemen worked miracles.

When the young ladies left their father, they moved to the parlor for tea. Mr. Collins sat in their father's chair, glaring at the young women seated around the tea table. After delivering him his cup of tea, they ignored him, enjoying the new camaraderie which sprang up among them. Mr. Bennet, remembering his promise to his daughters, joined them for tea and to keep an eye on Mr. Collins. On quiet feet, he arrived in the doorway. He noted the glare Mr. Collins cast upon his daughters. He heard muttering, but the words were too indistinct to understand. A look came into his cousin's eyes that Mr. Bennet did not like at all.

Mr. Collins stood, walked towards the tea table, and pretended to trip, dumping his still-full cup down the front of Elizabeth's gown. Uttering abject apologies, he retrieved a handkerchief from his pocket and leaned down, extending it towards Elizabeth's bosom. Elizabeth turned away so that his hand landed on her shoulder, just as her father's voice rang out, "Mr. Collins, what do you think you are doing?"

"My apologies, Mr. Bennet, I did not mean to drench Miss Elizabeth with tea. I was only trying to help.

"A gentleman may offer his hankie, but your attempts to brush at the stain were highly inappropriate. Were you attempting to compromise my daughter?" The gentleman demurred, but his tone was utterly insincere. "I believe, Mr. Collins, that you have overstayed your welcome. You should pack your bags and plan to depart in the morning."

"I am your heir and you are throwing me out of my future home."

"Yes, I am. I am uncomfortable with your behavior around my daughters of late and I doubt your ability to be trusted near them. You will need to walk into Meryton to arrange your transportation, but you will depart before breakfast in the morning. Do I make myself clear?"

"You and your ungrateful daughters will regret this one day when I inherit this house. I will not tolerate such treatment and will not hesitate to correct the behaviors which you have too long ignored. Your youngest daughters are nothing less than trollops, and I will return them to the schoolroom. Moreover, the utter disrespect I received from others of your daughters will be repaid in kind." The man glared at Elizabeth as he spoke.

"That is quite enough, Mr. Collins. Just to be clear, you will control Longbourn upon my death, but that will be the limit of your inheritance. My daughters will be left to the guardianship of others so that you will have no say in their futures."

"You cannot do that. I am their closest male relation."

"You are a very distant cousin and far from their closest male relation."

"Mark my words, you will regret this—all of you!" Mr. Collins said with another glare at Elizabeth. She rolled her eyes at the man's ridiculousness.

"I believe I shall make Mr. Darcy and his godfather, the bishop, aware of the threats you have made," said Mr. Bennet. "If you survive being called out by Mr. Darcy and his cousin, I hope you enjoy your new parish, if you even receive one."

Mr. Collins marched from the room. He had stopped to don his outerwear when Mr. Bennet appeared in the sitting room door. "By the way, I will have Mrs. Hill bring a tray to your room for supper. You are to avoid my daughters completely. It is not necessary to even take your leave of them."

Mr. Collins replied with a hate-filled glare before slamming the door behind him as he exited the house.

"I believe I will send a note to Mr. Darcy and the colonel. Do you wish to include a note with mine, Lizzy?"

"Yes, Papa. Thank you. I will do it now and bring it to your study."

Elizabeth rushed up to her room, sat at her desk, and dashed off a note to William.

Less than an hour later, Dawson, the Netherfield butler, approached Darcy with a letter on a salver as the party awaited the call to dinner. Excusing himself, Mr. Darcy stepped across the hall to the dining room to read the message in private.

"The blasted fool," Darcy ground out through gritted teeth.

"Who is a fool, cousin?"

"Mr. Collins. He attempted to put his hands on Elizabeth in front of her sisters. I will tear him limb from limb." Darcy opened the second note that was enclosed. When he finished, he growled, "Strike that. I will kill the man and then report him to my godfather!"

"Do you wish to eat first or should we pay the parson a visit?"

"I think we need to deal with that sniveling parson," declared Darcy. They saw the butler passing through the hall, likely preparing to announce dinner. Stopping Dawson, Darcy said, "Please have horses prepared immediately for the colonel and me." Darcy stepped into the drawing room and announced, "Richard and I will not be able to join you for dinner. Something has come up and we must take care of it immediately."

"Can it not wait until after dinner, Mr. Darcy?" whined Caroline. "You were gone most of the day and now you shall not dine with us. What on earth is so important?"

"No, it cannot wait. I am sorry for any inconvenience, Bingley."

"It is no problem, Darcy. I hope you can resolve the problem, whatever it is."

With a chuckle, the colonel replied, "It is nothing we cannot handle. Please excuse us."

Frustrated at Mr. Darcy's sudden departure, Caroline stalked from the room. Crossing the hall, she noted a paper on the sideboard in the dining room. Mr. Darcy, in his frustration, had left the notes behind. Wondering what might have caused the gentlemen to depart in such a rush, Caroline picked up the message on top. The handwriting was feminine but did not look like Georgiana's. Glancing at the bottom, she saw that the note was from Elizabeth Bennet. Why would she be writing to Mr. Darcy? Glancing over the letter, Caroline could not believe what she saw written on the page. Why would Darcy care about this? Accepting her father's heir would be the best Miss Elizabeth could expect. Was she playing on Darcy's honor as a gentleman, trying to secure him for herself? She folded the notes and gave them to Dawson. "Please give these to Mr. Darcy's valet. How much longer until dinner?"

"It is ready to be served now, miss."

"Please announce it to the others before you return the notes."

Caroline allowed the footman to seat her. She would have to learn what Miss Elizabeth was up to and why Mr. Darcy reacted as he did.

# CONSEQUENCES FOR MR. COLLINS

AS DARCY AND RICHARD RACED TO Longbourn, they came across the hapless Mr. Collins dragging his trunk along the street, headed for the inn. Darcy reined in his horse and jumped down in front of the parson. Without a word, he pulled back his arm and planted the ridiculous man a facer. Mr. Collins sprawled into the dirt of the road. Stunned, he lay there, rubbing his jaw.

"What are you about, Mr. Darcy?"

"After your behavior and the threats you made to Miss Elizabeth and her family, you should not need to ask. You may be assured, sir, that my godfather will learn of your inappropriate behavior. I will ensure that you are removed from your post at Hunsford and sent somewhere much less appealing."

"I doubt you shall be successful in your desires, Mr. Darcy. I am certain that Lady Catherine shall protect me, especially when she learns that I was attempting to protect her daughter's interests."

Darcy punched the now-seated gentleman again, then kicked him for good measure. Mr. Collins fell back onto the dirt road. "Just remember my promise, Mr. Collins. Meddle in my life and I will call you out. If you fail to face me, I will denounce you for the coward and scoundrel that you are."

Collins' face paled, but he stared at the gentleman. "You do not frighten me, Mr. Darcy. Right is on my side."

As Darcy pulled back his arm to strike the man again, Richard grabbed it and stopped him. "He is not worth the trouble, Darcy. There are others far more important at the moment than this cretin."

"You are right, Richard. Let us leave the rubbish in the street where it belongs." Darcy remounted and they kicked their horses into a gallop, showering Collins with dirt as they rode away without a backward look.

Mr. Collins noted the crowd that had gathered during his confrontation with Mr. Darcy. He replaced his hat on his head and attempted to stand. Losing his balance, he fell back into the street. Collins looked around, waiting for someone to come to his aid, but most of those who stood to observe the altercation turned their backs on Mr. Collins and went about their business. The longer he sat, the angrier he became. After getting on his feet, he managed to drag his trunk to the inn.

"I need a room for the night."

"I'm 'fraid I'm full up," grumbled the innkeeper.

"In a small town like this, how can that be?"

"I said I'm full up. You can sleep in the common room if you want."

"When is the next coach to London?"

"It comes through at seven tomorrow mornin'."

"Can I get some dinner?"

"Can you pay for it?" questioned the innkeeper rudely.

"Do you not offer consideration for a parson?"

"Why should I offer you any consideration? I 'eard what Mr. Darcy said about you makin' threats to Miss Elizabeth and her family. We don't take kindly 'round here to men who mistreat young ladies, 'specially young ladies as kind as Miss Elizabeth. Now, can you pay for a meal or not?"

Mr. Collins pulled a small purse from his pocket and looked inside. "How much will the coach fare be to London, then to Hunsford?" The innkeeper quoted the price for the trip to London, but could not tell him how much more it would be for the second leg of his trip. Looking back at the money in his pouch, Collins said, "Bring me a pint and some bread and cheese. I must be sure that I can get back to my parish. I shall, however, warn others of my calling to avoid such an inhospitable place." Mr. Collins turned to walk away, leaving his trunk in the hall.

"Don't leave that in the way of my paying customers," called the innkeeper, "or it will find its way to the garbage."

With a huff, Mr. Collins grabbed the handle of the heavy trunk and dragged it along behind him. He selected a table in the corner near the fire and pushed the chest against the wall. Deciding that the easiest way to watch his belongings should he fall asleep would be to use the trunk for his chair, he settled down on the hard surface, then leaned back against the wall.

As he waited for the serving wench to bring his meal, he wondered if he should write to his patroness. However, he decided the evidence of her nephew's beating, would give weight to his words about Darcy being seduced from his obligations to her daughter.

For the remainder of the ride to Longbourn, William was silent, though Richard sensed he was deep in thought. As they drew close to the turnoff for the estate, Richard said, "I do not want to rush you, but if you plan to continue this relationship, you might want to accelerate your plans so as to preempt any actions Aunt Catherine will take after hearing Mr. Collins' tale."

"Miss Elizabeth is the most remarkable woman I have ever met. I very much wanted to enjoy this period of courtship with her for both our sakes. However, I admit I do not want to lose Miss Elizabeth or subject her to Aunt Catherine's *tender* mercies. What if she is not ready to move forward so soon?"

"I doubt you need to worry about that. Anyone who looks at the two of you can see that Miss Elizabeth returns your feelings. Why do you not talk to Elizabeth when we arrive? I will get the story from Mr. Bennet."

"Thank you, Richard, I appreciate your support. What do you think will be your parents' opinion of Elizabeth?"

"You know the only thing they ever wanted was your happiness. They may be surprised at first, but I am certain they will be accepting of Elizabeth, particularly when they see how happy you are with each other." Richard grinned at his cousin, prompting a grin from Darcy as well.

When the gentlemen arrived at Longbourn, they separated, each to his assigned task.

William joined the sisters in the sitting room, with an apology that Mrs. Bennet had retired due to her nerves. With a whispered word to Elizabeth, he was able to separate her from her sisters. They moved into the room where the pianoforte rested. Elizabeth sat at the keyboard and picked out a song she could play without the music so that their conversation would not be overheard and so that no one would be tempted to interrupt them. William sat beside her on the bench as she played.

"Are you well, Elizabeth?" His voice was soft and filled with concern.

"I am well, Mr. Darcy. Mr. Collins was unsuccessful in his attempt to compromise me. However, he did do some good while he was here."

"I cannot imagine what good that buffoon could do anyone. In fact, I feel sorry for his parishioners."

"I cannot disagree with you about those in his care, but his vile behavior helped my younger sisters understand the danger of their flirtatious behavior and how it would affect the whole family."

"He did not lay hands on you, did he? I already informed him of my displeasure," said Darcy, unconsciously rubbing his knuckles. "However, if he so much as touched one hair on your head, I will not hesitate to follow through and call him out."

Elizabeth had seen the way Darcy touched his hand and noticed the redness of his fist. She wondered what he had done and secretly hoped he had left an impression her contemptible cousin would not soon forget. "He tried but was unsuccessful."

"Knowing that Mr. Collins' actions could have caused me to lose you—at least to his mind—made me realize that I wish to spend the rest of my life with you. I know our relationship is not of long duration, but I know that you are the only woman I can imagine spending the rest of my life with." Darcy paused to look deeply into Elizabeth's eyes. "I love you and hope you will accept my hand in marriage."

Elizabeth's eyes were wide and glistened with tears. She opened her mouth to speak, but no words would come. Taking a deep breath, she picked up his injured hand and brushed her lips across his knuckles. "Did you do this for me?"

Darcy only smiled.

"After your heroic actions, how could I say anything other than yes?" Darcy's smile showed his dimples, but before he had time to speak, Elizabeth added, "I love you as well, William."

"May I kiss you, Elizabeth?" She peeked around him and did not see any of her sisters, so she nodded. William lifted one hand to cup her cheek and slid the other around her waist, drawing her closer. He lowered his head until their lips met gently. Darcy gradually increased the pressure, drawing away only when they needed to breathe. They rested their foreheads together as their breathing calmed. "I should talk to your father. If he gives his consent, I would like to send the notice to the Times about our engagement tonight. When I confronted Mr. Collins, he was under the impression that my aunt can and will protect him from anything I might attempt to do. He is wrong, but I do not want to give him the opportunity to paint you in a bad light. Nor do I want my aunt to think she can control my life. She can do nothing once we announce our engagement."

"Is she the only one in your family likely to object to our engagement?" asked Elizabeth. Darcy did not like to hear the lack of confidence in her voice. "What will your sister think? Do you think she will like me?"

"Elizabeth, Georgiana will love having you for a sister. You are just what she needs."

"What about the earl and countess? Will they accept me?"

"The only thing my aunt and uncle desire is my happiness. They never supported Lady Catherine's demand that I marry her daughter. Even my cousin, Anne, does not wish to marry me. There is nothing about which you need to worry. Please remember, I am the head of the Darcy family. I am accountable to no one, and you are the woman with whom I wish to share my life."

"Thank you, William, for reassuring me. I will wait to share the news with my sisters until you gain Papa's permission." With one more quick kiss, they rejoined the others. Darcy excused himself from the sisters.

Meanwhile, in Mr. Bennet's study, Colonel Fitzwilliam recounted their encounter with Mr. Collins in the streets of Meryton. Richard's flair for storytelling had the older gentleman chuckling. "Unfortunately, sir, I do not believe Mr. Collins is through with his attempts to cause trouble. His lack of sense is so great that he believes my aunt has the power to protect him from any actions anyone might take against him."

"Does Lady Catherine have such power?"

"No, indeed, Mr. Bennet, she does not. Despite Mr. Collins' veneration of my aunt, other than her rather forceful demeanor, she is somewhat of a recluse who has not been to London for many seasons. She is the daughter of an earl, which gives her an inflated opinion of her importance. That same conviction in her background makes her think that she still wields power. However, she is so opinionated that Lady Catherine alienates everyone she has ever known."

"Lady Catherine sounds as entertaining in her own way as Mr. Collins."

"You might be the only person who sees her as entertaining. Most in the family find her infuriating, vexatious, or downright dreadful."

Their laughter was interrupted by a knock at the door.

"Come," called Mr. Bennet.

Darcy entered with a questioning gaze at his cousin. He directed his comment to Mr. Bennet. "I am surprised to hear laughter after the day you endured."

"Like my Lizzy, my temper flares in the moment, but I never fail to see the humor in a situation. That is what makes life tolerable, Mr. Darcy."

"I look forward to hearing Miss Elizabeth's laughter often in the future. In fact, I would like to speak to you for a moment, Mr. Bennet."

"Would you like me to leave, Darcy?"

"Would you mind giving us a few moments, Richard?"

"Not at all. I shall entertain the ladies while you gentlemen talk." With a bow to Mr. Bennet, Richard left the room and closed the door behind him.

Mr. Bennet waved the young man to a seat in front of his desk. "Please take a seat, Mr. Darcy. What did you wish to speak to me about?"

"Mr. Bennet, I know that my acquaintance with your daughter is not of long duration. However, Mr. Collins' actions caused me to realize that I might have lost her. I asked Miss Elizabeth to marry me. She accepted and we would like to ask for your blessing and consent."

"I knew this day might come but I did not imagine that my Lizzy would be lucky enough to find a man who was worthy of her. I grant my consent and blessing. I hope that you will bring her back to visit often."

Upon receiving the desired response, Darcy smiled his dimpled smile. "Before we share the good news, I would like to let you know that I wish to send the announcement of our engagement to the papers immediately."

"Is there a reason for the rush?"

"I do not believe that Mr. Collins will heed my warning to keep my business from my aunt. The announcement of our engagement will prevent any attempts at mischief she might make."

Mr. Bennet was quiet for a moment. "I see that you are a man of forethought and determination. I believe you will need both of those traits in a marriage with my Lizzy. I hope you realize the value of a woman like her."

"I do indeed, Mr. Bennet. I shall dedicate my life to her happiness and well-being."

"In that case, shall we share the good news?"

Darcy nodded.

"You are fortunate that Mrs. Bennet has retired, for you are spared her joyous effusions."

The gentlemen returned to the sitting room. Darcy hurried to Elizabeth's side. Mr. Bennet remained in the doorway and called for everyone's attention. When all eyes were upon him, Mr. Bennet said, "It gives me great pleasure to announce the engagement of Elizabeth and Mr. Darcy."

Elizabeth's sisters rushed to surround her, and the colonel slapped his cousin on the back, wishing him a hearty congratulations. When the excitement died down, Elizabeth walked the gentlemen to the door. After the colonel exited, Darcy stole a quick kiss and departed with a promise to visit in the morning.

When Darcy and Richard returned to Netherfield, Bingley met them in the foyer. "Were you able to take care of the emergency?"

"Yes, there was a satisfying resolution," replied Darcy with a wide grin.

Surprised at his friend's expression, Bingley remarked, "Why don't you take a dinner tray in my study and tell me all about it?" After Bingley gave instructions to a passing footman, the men settled in the study. Bingley poured a brandy for each of them. They chatted of estate matters until the housekeeper and a maid arrived with trays for the gentlemen, who had missed dinner. When the servants departed, Richard told Bingley of the note from Mr. Bennet and the trouble Mr. Collins had attempted to make. He recounted the encounter with Mr. Collins in the streets of Meryton and their arrival at Longbourn. "However, I believe the best news of the evening is Darcy's to share."

"Better than punishing the cad with your fists?" asked Bingley.

"Better by far."

"Tell me, man, what is this news?"

"I asked Miss Elizabeth to marry me and she accepted. We received Mr. Bennet's permission. The announcement is already on its way to the Times by an express rider."

On the other side of the door, Caroline Bingley covered her mouth with her hand to prevent a gasp of dismay from escaping. Having heard Mr. Darcy and the colonel return earlier, Caroline had begun to walk about the room, pausing beside the drawing room door in the hopes of overhearing their conversation. Catching only her brother's instructions to the servant, she had excused herself from the drawing room. When the footman had disappeared from the hall to deliver the message to the housekeeper, Caroline had found a dark corner of the hall, where she had remained out of sight until the servants departed the study. With a furtive look around the hall, she had sneaked to the door of the study and placed her ear against the smooth surface. Now she might have a chance to understand why Miss Eliza's note had caused such a strong reaction in Mr. Darcy.

Fortunately for her, the colonel's voice was loud and easily understood through the thick wood. Her eyes had grown wide at Mr. Collins' attempted compromise, but Caroline truly believed that Miss Elizabeth could expect nothing better.

Now it was Darcy's voice speaking. His low tones were quieter, but that did not make his words less shocking. Caroline could not believe what Darcy had said. Perhaps she misunderstood, but that hope shattered when her brother's shout of congratulations rang through the door.

Having heard more than she wished, Caroline stepped away from the door and rushed up the stairs to her room. She may have accepted the fact that Mr. Darcy would never marry her, but Caroline refused to allow that impertinent country chit to succeed where she had failed. *How can I prevent this travesty? There must be something I can do.* It was these thoughts that swirled through her mind as sleep claimed her.

# RETURN TO KENT

IT HAD TAKEN MR. COLLINS TWO full days to return home, as he had missed the connecting coach in London that would return him to Kent. Then the coach had stopped so many times that it was too late to call on Rosings when he arrived. Consequently, on the fourth day after his expulsion from Longbourn, Mr. Collins presented himself at Rosings Park to advise Lady Catherine of his return. It secretly pleased him that the bruises on his face showed the most vibrant colors. With his cut lip and black eye, he could not fail to garner sympathy from his patroness. Affecting a limp, Mr. Collins entered the room, where Lady Catherine waited for him.

"What on earth happened to you, Mr. Collins? You know that I do not approve of physical violence."

"I am sorry to report, your ladyship, that your nephew, Mr. Fitzwilliam Darcy, caused these injuries."

"Do not be ridiculous, Mr. Collins. What do you know of my nephew?"

"I had the opportunity, or perhaps I should say misfortune, to meet your nephew in Hertfordshire. He was visiting an estate that borders my inheritance."

"How dare you accuse my nephew of such ungentlemanly behavior? Darcy would never act as you say," declared Lady Catherine in disgust.

"Perhaps under normal circumstances, my lady, but I fear he is bewitched. I arrived at my cousin's home to discover the eldest of the young ladies is already being courted. The second of my cousins appeared to be drab and ill-mannered. The third daughter was presentable, fond of the scriptures, and plays the pianoforte quite well, so I directed my attention to her for almost a week. However, on my first Friday there, the second daughter, who is, in reality, very beautiful, came downstairs to join the family, looking like her true self. Before an opportunity came to approach her, a visiting militia officer swooped in and monopolized her attention. Then two more visitors arrived in the persons of your nephews, Mr. Darcy and Colonel Fitzwilliam. After they routed the officer who had approached Miss Elizabeth, the second sister, Mr. Bennet announced the courtship of Mr. Darcy and Miss Elizabeth. I tried to impress upon them the fact that the courtship could not stand, as Mr. Darcy had a previous engagement to your daughter. Mr. Darcy and the colonel both denied the existence of any engagement, saying it was only your wish and that it was not official and never would be." Mr. Collins used all of the limited acting skills he possessed to guarantee a spirited reaction from Lady Catherine.

"Darcy would never do such a thing, Mr. Collins. You must be mistaken."

"I wish that I were, your ladyship, but both gentlemen threatened to call me out if I said such a thing to anyone else."

"Is that when you received these injuries?"

"No, that occurred later."

"What else took place?" asked Lady Catherine, doubt creeping into her voice.

"I tried to convince Miss Elizabeth to break the engagement, but she would not agree, though I offered her marriage in Mr. Darcy's place. She told her father that I tried to compromise her and he most likely relayed the story to Mr. Darcy. Mr. Bennet threw me out of the house and forced me to walk, dragging my trunk, into the village to take the coach back to Hunsford. Before I arrived at the inn, I encountered Mr. Darcy and the colonel. Your nephew used his fists to make me aware of his displeasure. I tried to explain to him what had occurred, but he refused to believe me and threatened to call me out again. Finally, Colonel Fitzwilliam pulled him away and they left me beaten in the street."

By this time, Lady Catherine was seething with anger. "Darcy would not dare go against me in this way. He knows it was the greatest wish of his mother and myself that he and Anne marry. It looks as if I must take matters into my own hands. I will put a stop to this courtship by sending an announcement to the paper of the engagement. After that, I will expect you to return to Hertfordshire and marry that little hussy. I shall delight in having her under my control and I will be sure she understands her place in the world."

Mr. Collins bowed his head to hide his smile of pleasure at Lady Catherine's words.

"Please leave, Mr. Collins. I do not wish to see you again until your face returns to normal. Your injuries cause me anger and discomfort."

"Of course, your ladyship," said Mr. Collins as he backed from the room.

Unfortunately for Lady Catherine, she was in for a great shock. After writing the announcement to the Times of Darcy and Anne's engagement, she sat down to read the morning post. As she perused the announcements column while dreaming of viewing the one she had just sent off to the paper, a notice caught her eye.

Engaged: Mr. Fitzwilliam Darcy of Darcy House and Pemberley to Miss Elizabeth Diana Bennet, daughter of Mr. and Mrs. Thomas Bennet of Longbourn, Hertfordshire. The couple plans to marry early in the new year.

After reading the announcement, Lady Catherine screamed in rage and frustration. Her shouts brought her daughter, the butler, and the housekeeper running.

"What is wrong, Mama?" cried Anne, slightly out of breath.

"Madame, how can I assist you?" asked the butler.

The housekeeper held out a vinaigrette to her mistress but did not speak.

"I need my carriage made ready right away. Have my maid begin packing. I must be on my way to London as soon as possible, preferably within the hour. We will stop to see my brother the earl before continuing to Hertfordshire.

"What is in Hertfordshire, Mama?"

"Your cousin, Darcy. I plan to convince him to return with me so that we might announce your engagement."

"Mama, Darcy and I both told you we do not wish to wed. Why are you so set on this?"

"Because you deserve to be the next mistress of Pemberley. I named you after my sister, and you should follow in her footsteps."

"You always tell me I am too weak to manage Rosings or help make decisions for the estate. William was forced to shoulder a great many burdens at a young age. Why would you wish to add to those burdens by saddling him with a wife he must take care of rather than one who can ease his concerns and care for his estate? Please, Mama, for my sake, let go of this matter."

Lady Catherine was shocked at her daughter's words. "I did not think you serious when you said you did not wish to marry Darcy. I thought you were just trying to appease your cousin with your words."

"No, Mama. I love William. He is a wonderful cousin, but we are not suited to one another. We are both quiet and reserved. Each of us must marry someone who will bring laughter and joy to our lives. We could not do that for each other. I want William to find the happiness he deserves, and that would not be with me. If he found someone to make him happy, please allow him that experience."

"You are sure you do not wish to marry Darcy?"

"No, Mama, I do not. I have always preferred Richard to William. He makes me happy, and he makes me laugh. That is what I want for my future. I do not know if he feels the same way, but I plan to leave Rosings Park to Richard when I pass away. I want him to be able to resign from the army. I want him home and safe."

"Do you wish me to mention the possibility of your marrying Richard to your uncle? I want you to be happy, my child."

"If Richard is interested, I would be pleased to marry him, but promise me you will not force him into a marriage he does not want. It is probably not fair for me to marry anyone. I doubt I will be able to provide my husband with an heir."

"If you wish, we will seek a new doctor. I know that I never wanted to do so before, but perhaps your uncle can suggest one. Perhaps there can be more to your future than you believe. I will do whatever I can for your happiness, my dear daughter."

"Then do not go to Hertfordshire. Send Darcy a letter wishing him well and welcoming his betrothed to the family. That would make me happy."

Lady Catherine stared at her daughter for a long time. It was hard to let go of her dreams, but all she ever desired was what was best for Anne. If this was what she wanted, Lady Catherine would agree. "It will be as you desire, Anne." She turned to the butler, who stood poised in the doorway to carry out his mistress's wishes. "If you delivered my earlier orders, please cancel them. I shall not be traveling at this time after all. Now, if you will excuse me, I have some letters to write." Her posture stiff and straight, but her steps somewhat slower, Lady Catherine retired to her study.

At the parsonage, Mr. Collins' mail had also arrived. As he looked through the letters, he was surprised to find one written in an unknown feminine hand.

"I tried to tell her he would not follow through with a proposal," sneered Mr. Collins. Perhaps I should leave her to wither on the shelf. After the way she treated me, it is all she deserves." Then he recalled Lady Catherine's words and did not wish to incur her wrath. Before he broke the seal on the letter, a knock came at the door. A footman in the Rosings livery handed him a note before turning to leave. Mr. Collins unfolded the paper and quickly scanned the contents. The longer he read, the more his face fell until his expression ultimately resembled a scowl.

How could this have happened? Why would Lady Catherine give up on her desires for her daughter to marry Darcy? How was he to gain control of Elizabeth if Darcy were permitted to marry her? What could he do to achieve his desires and not cause his patroness to be angry with him?

It was then that he recalled the other letter. After rapidly breaking the seal, Mr. Collins began to read. This time, his expression changed to one of evil. His eyes were cold and his grin broad. His laughter would raise the hair on the back of one's neck. He sat at the desk in his study and hurried to pen his reply.

# MEETING GEORGIANA

WITHIN A WEEK OF THE ANNOUNCEMENT of his engagement appearing in the paper, Darcy received a stack of letters. Georgiana's contained excitement and concern about her brother's betrothal. She was happy he had found someone to love but worried that Miss Elizabeth would not like her or would judge her for her poor choices with Wickham. The letter also contained her travel plans for the trip to Netherfield. Richard sent his hearty congratulations. The Earl and Countess of Matlock sent their congratulations, which were tempered by concern about Elizabeth's background. Darcy received a letter from Anne full of good wishes for his future happiness. The most surprising correspondence of all came from his Aunt Catherine.

*Rosings Park*
*Kent*
*November 22, 1811*

*Dear Darcy,*

*I am pleased to learn of your engagement and hope you and your young lady will be very happy.*

*Upon hearing Mr. Collins' tale and then reading the announcement, I was furious. However, a conversation with Anne helped me to understand that marriage to each other is not what would be best for either of you.*

*I am concerned that the young lady comes from such a low sphere that she could be related to my parson. I hope the young woman you selected will not be an embarrassment to the Fitzwilliam family and name.*

*After you have settled in, you must bring the young woman to visit. I will instruct her in anything that she needs to know to be the mistress of Pemberley.*

*Lady Catherine de Bourgh*

To say that his aunt's words shocked Darcy would be a tremendous understatement. Could it possibly be true that she has given up on her designs for Anne and me? Or is Aunt Catherine attempting to lure me into a false sense of security or a trap? He reread Anne's letter and found that she also mentioned her mother's capitulation and believed her sincere.

Two days before the Bingleys' ball, Georgiana Darcy and Colonel Fitzwilliam arrived at Netherfield Park. Bingley invited Jane and Elizabeth to come for afternoon tea, thereby giving Georgiana time to rest after her travels as well as to meet Elizabeth for the first time without the chaos that ruled at Longbourn. As teatime approached, a nervous Georgiana sat in the largest drawing room with all the residents of the manor house, waiting for the visitors.

Georgiana noted with pleasant surprise that Miss Bingley was not as solicitous of her as usual. She was a bit more supercilious, however.

"My dear Miss Darcy, I would suggest you not raise your expectations too high. The Bennet sisters, though pleasant enough, are nothing compared to your friends and relations in the first circles." Though abiding by her brother's strictures regarding their neighbors, the tone of Caroline's voice gave the lie to her words.

Georgiana was surprised at her words and uncertain how to respond. She finally managed to say, "Ah, why, thank you, Miss Bingley." She glanced at William to see if he found her response appropriate only to catch him rolling his eyes at Richard. Georgiana was forced to look down to hide the smile her brother's actions elicited.

Miss Darcy had barely managed to compose herself before Dawson appeared in the doorway and announced, "Miss Bennet and Miss Elizabeth Bennet."

Charles hurried to greet the ladies as they entered the room. Darcy stood as well, his bright smile only for Elizabeth.

"Miss Bennet, Miss Elizabeth, we are glad you could join us this afternoon."

"Indeed, we are," said Darcy. "Elizabeth, I believe you remember the colonel. Please allow me to introduce you to my sister, Miss Georgiana Darcy. Georgie, this is my betrothed, Miss Elizabeth Bennet, and her elder sister, Miss Bennet." The ladies curtsied to each other upon introduction and murmured the usual words. Darcy and Elizabeth joined Georgiana on the settee so that the girls could speak and become better acquainted. Jane and Charles settled nearby.

Having been removed as hostess by her brother when she had complained about arranging the ball, Caroline waited with the others to receive her tea. She was not close enough to participate in any of the conversations in the room but studied the others carefully. Accepting that Darcy honestly would not ever marry her, she was resigned to moving on when next in London for the season. Understanding, however, did not mean that she was willing to allow the young lady he selected to be someone she considered far below herself in social status. If he was willing to accept a nobody like Eliza Bennet, how could a tradesman's daughter be that different? Caroline still did not understand that it was her personality more than her status that made her an unwanted candidate. As such, she would arrange things so that Miss Elizabeth would not be an acceptable candidate, either.

While Caroline studied the others present, Elizabeth did her best to get to know Miss Darcy. It was immediately apparent to Elizabeth that Miss Darcy was shy and very uncertain of herself.

"I am very pleased you were able to join us, Miss Darcy. Will you be attending the ball that Mr. Bingley is holding?"

"I am very pleased to be here, Miss Elizabeth. I do not often get to join William on his travels. However, as I am not out yet, I will not attend the ball."

Elizabeth looked beyond Georgiana to catch Darcy's eye. Her raised brow and expression easily allowed Darcy to understand her question.

"If you would like to attend with Mrs. Annesley, though you will not be able to dance, you might do so, Georgie."

Her eyes widened in surprise and delight. "I would like that very much, William." Miss Darcy hesitated and a bright blush appeared on her cheeks. "Might I dance with you and Richard as practice before my debut?"

Elizabeth's eyes sparkled at her future sister's request, which brought a grin to both Darcy's and Richard's faces. The cousins looked at each other. At Richard's grinning nod, Darcy said, "I believe that would be acceptable. If Charles is willing, I might even extend the list of acceptable partners to include Mr. Bingley as well."

"I would be happy to partner Miss Darcy," said Charles. "As the host, it is my duty—if, perhaps, not my preference—to dance with all the young ladies in attendance." His eyes drifted to Jane as he spoke, but she only smiled serenely.

The gentlemen took a few minutes to request their sets. Soon, Jane, Elizabeth, and Georgiana were each engaged for the first three sets.

"I am glad you are excited to attend the ball. It is not the attitude I usually have for such events. However, I believe it would be best if you retired after dinner."

"Thank you so much, William. I am happy to agree with your request. And thank you, Miss Elizabeth. I am sure you had something to do with William's decision. I believe I will like having you for a sister very much!"

"Well, then, if we are to be sisters, you must call me Elizabeth or Lizzy, as my family does."

"Thank you, Lizzy, and will you call me Georgiana or Georgie, as William and Richard do?"

"It would be my pleasure, Georgie."

As she overheard this portion of their conversation, Miss Bingley's anger increased. She had never been offered this familiarity and she had known Miss Darcy for several years.

Georgiana and the two couples continued to speak for some time, with occasional input from Mrs. Hurst, while her husband snored in a chair in the corner of the room.

Darcy was very much enjoying the afternoon. With pleasure, he watched the ease with which Georgiana and Elizabeth spoke. However, he could not remember the last time he had been in the same room as Miss Bingley for so long without her attempting to dominate the conversation. Not only did she not try to control the conversation, but she said not a word. Her behavior made Darcy uneasy.

Before departing, Jane invited everyone to take tea at Longbourn on the morrow.

Upon returning to Netherfield after the tea at Longbourn, Georgiana rushed up the stairs towards her chambers.

"Are you well, Georgie?" called William in concern. "Come, little mouse, sit with us and let us talk."

Without looking back, Georgiana said, "Perhaps in a little while. I must refresh myself first."

Mrs. Annesley understood her charge's upset. Turning, she gave her employer a nod and a smile, letting him know that she would watch over and care for Miss Darcy.

Once in the safety of her sitting room, Georgiana threw herself into a chair, unable to speak. The event had started well, though she had been a bit overwhelmed by the exuberance of Mrs. Bennet. Her younger daughters were only slightly less effusive in their welcome and behavior. Georgiana was surprised at how different Miss Bennet and Miss Elizabeth were from the others. However, as she thought about it, she realized that Richard was entirely different from his elder brother. Considering more about the Bennet sisters, Georgiana recognized that there was something she could relate to with each one, despite their apparent differences. She and Miss Mary both enjoyed the pianoforte and music, while she and Miss Kitty shared a love of drawing. It was what Miss Lydia told her that caused Georgiana's distress. She had mentioned the militia soldiers in Meryton and how charming she found Lieutenant George Wickham. Lydia did not notice the way the color had drained from Georgiana's face as she continued to explain that he had been arrested in the very room in which they sat.

Mrs. Annesley watched as the various emotions flickered across her charge's face. Miss Darcy comported herself well considering the shock she had received. *Perhaps I should check on her.*

"Miss Darcy, are you feeling calmer? You handled the shock well. Not even your brother and cousin are aware of what happened."

Georgiana's deep sigh reached her companion's ears. "Are you sure no one observed anything?"

"I believe so. Miss Elizabeth might have noticed something, but I think her only concern was for your well-being."

"Do you think my brother would tell Lizzy about Wickham?"

"He may have felt honor-bound to discuss it, as they are to marry."

Georgiana nodded in understanding. "I hope that Lizzy does not think poorly of me for my mistakes."

"Miss Elizabeth was kindness itself yesterday. I do not think you need to worry about that, Miss Darcy."

A short time later, a knock at the door interrupted the ladies' conversation. Mrs. Annesley answered and admitted Mr. Darcy and Colonel Fitzwilliam. She took the opportunity to request tea for the group.

"Georgiana, are you well? What happened that you would not speak on your return from Longbourn? Did someone upset you? Please tell me what is wrong," cried a worried Darcy.

"I am sorry to cause you concern, William. It is just that I was taken by surprise when Miss Lydia mentioned an attraction to George Wickham, and then to learn of his arrest."

"Oh, forgive me–"

"Us," piped in Richard.

"Georgie, I should have told you about his presence in the area."

"He did not harm any of the Bennets, did he?"

"No, but not for a lack of trying."

"Will you tell me what happened and what has become of him?

"When I returned from London, I found Wickham ensconced in the Bennets' sitting room. Upon his arrival, he had sat next to Miss Elizabeth and told her his tale of woe at my hands. However, Elizabeth did not believe it. She went to discuss the matter with her father and met me in the hall when Richard and I arrived. She alerted me to Wickham's presence and what he had said. Richard and I determined the best way to deal with him and entered the room.

"It was rather fun to see the man squirm. He tried to sneak out, but I couldn't allow that," laughed Richard. "I clamped my hand firmly on his shoulder and proceeded to alert all those present about his past behavior." Georgiana paled at his words, so Richard quickly added, "Though no mention was made of you, of course."

Changing the subject as rapidly as possible, Darcy said, "Before we entered the sitting room, I asked Mr. Bennet to send someone for the magistrate. By the time Richard was finished with Wickham's past, I had announced that I carried all of his debts with me and would arrange for him to be arrested and sent to Marshalsea. Wickham is now in debtor's prison and will not see the light of day until he is old and gray."

"If he survives that long," muttered Richard.

At that moment came a knock on the door. A servant entered with a tea tray. "I thought a little refreshment might help you with the discussion, Miss Darcy."

"Thank you for your thoughtfulness, Mrs. Annesley."

"Have you decided which gown you will wear for the ball tomorrow?" Darcy asked.

"I thought the soft rose one, but I must go into the village tomorrow to look for some ribbons that will match or complement it."

"What time would you like to depart for the village? Perhaps you, Richard, and I could ride in the morning."

"That sounds delightful, William. We should leave by ten so that we will all have time to rest and prepare in the afternoon before the ball."

The men exchanged a look before the chuckles escaped. Soon they were laughing and holding their sides. Georgiana looked at her companions in confusion, only to see that Mrs. Annesley was attempting to contain a smile of her own.

"And just what is so funny?" asked an indignant Georgiana.

His sister's reaction only made the men laugh harder. "I believe, Miss Darcy, that they are laughing at the thought of needing to rest for more than a few minutes to prepare for a ball."

"So, you are laughing at me?" demanded Georgiana while trying to maintain her serious demeanor. "Well, if it were not for the fickleness of men, women would not have to work so hard to prepare. A young lady must work hard to stand out in a room full of other women." By this time, her smile was quite evident to the others.

"When young ladies are as lovely as you and Elizabeth, you need not worry too much about preparing. Your natural beauty shines through," said Darcy gallantly.

"Hear, hear!" cried Richard before they all dissolved into laughter again.

# THE NETHERFIELD BALL BEGINS

THE NEXT MORNING, ELIZABETH ESCAPED THE noise of her home with Mary. Elizabeth needed to purchase a ribbon for her hair to match a new dress. In her closet was the dress that had been purchased to replace the one Miss Bingley had ruined at the assembly. The dress had remained in Elizabeth's closet since it had arrived. She was waiting for the perfect opportunity to wear it and the Netherfield ball seemed like the ideal opportunity.

As she stood looking over the ribbons, a voice behind her called, "Good morning, Lizzy. What are you doing here?"

Turning to the voice, Elizabeth saw Georgiana enter in a riding habit. She was followed by Darcy and the colonel.

"Good morning, Georgiana, Mr. Darcy, Colonel Fitzwilliam."

"Good morning, Miss Elizabeth."

Darcy advanced to Elizabeth. Taking her hand, he held it in his own as he said, "Good morning, Elizabeth. I hope you are well." Then he bowed over the hand he held and placed a kiss on the back of it. "What a delightful surprise to see you this morning. It is an unexpected pleasure. Are you looking for something in particular?"

"Indeed. I recently received a new dress and I need some hair ribbons that will match it."

"That is what I am looking for as well."

"What color do you need, Georgiana?"

"Something to go with a pale rose color."

"What about you, Elizabeth?"

"I was looking for pale yellow and white." As Darcy took note of her choices, an idea occurred to him.

Darcy turned to Mary. "Are you searching for something as well, Miss Mary?"

"Not really. Dr. Fordyce does not think it appropriate for young women to take too much interest in their attire."

"I do not believe Mr. Fordyce would find it inappropriate for you to care for your appearance at a special event. He is simply cautioning young women against thinking of only their outward appearance and not the more important internal beauty. I do not know what color your gown is, but I believe the splendid light green ribbon would enhance your eyes and show off their natural beauty." Darcy pointed to the ribbon he meant.

Mary blushed at Mr. Darcy's words and said, "I never thought about it like that before. I thank you for your insight into the passage, Mr. Darcy. Perhaps I will make a purchase after all."

With much giggling, the girls helped each other make their selections as the gentleman observed them with fond expressions on their faces. When they exited the shop, the two groups took their leave of each other. Darcy could not pass up a chance to take Elizabeth's hand for another kiss.

"I shall be counting the moments until your arrival. I look forward to opening the ball with you, my lovely Elizabeth."

Color suffused her face, but Elizabeth did not look away. "I look forward to being in your arms again. Until then, my sweet William." Darcy's grin grew at her obvious affection. He could not wait for the time when he could kiss her without stopping and no longer have to separate at the end of the day.

As the Bennet carriage turned into the drive at Netherfield, the younger girls gaped at the sight of lit torches lining the drive. Every window of the house glowed with light. The torches showed the carriages which lined the drive, waiting to unload their passengers. Jane, Elizabeth, and Mary rode on the rear-facing seat, so each turned to the window to see what had caused the reaction from their younger sisters.

It took almost ten minutes before their carriage reached the main entrance. Footmen rushed forward, hands extended, to help the sisters exit. Lydia practically jumped over her sisters, trying to be the first to exit, but her father put out his arm to halt her progress.

"You, young lady, will follow your sisters, as is appropriate. Nothing will change in the few seconds you are behind them. You and Kitty have both improved somewhat in manners, and I hope it will continue tonight."

"Yes, Papa," said Lydia and Kitty at almost the same time.

Mr. Bennet stepped down, then helped his wife descend. Next, the patiently waiting footman assisted Jane, Elizabeth, Mary, Kitty, and Lydia in exiting. After a few minutes, the party stood before their hosts in the main hall of Netherfield.

"Good evening, Mr. and Mrs. Bennet. I am glad you could join us."

"We are delighted to be here," gushed Mrs. Bennet. "We are all excited about the ball."

The couple moved on and Bingley greeted Jane and Elizabeth. "Ladies, you both look lovely this evening," he commented gallantly. Mr. Bingley looked at Jane as he made his comment, but Elizabeth did not notice, as she was looking for William. Finally free from his distraction with the beauty before him, Bingley noticed her sister's actions. "I believe you will find Darcy waiting for you at the ballroom door." Elizabeth blushed but thanked Mr. Bingley for the information.

They moved on to his sisters. Mr. and Mrs. Hurst spoke pleasantly to both girls, as did Miss Bingley, whose greeting was a cause for wonderment. She spoke politely to both ladies, grudgingly complimented Elizabeth's gown, and hoped they would have a memorable evening. An almost knowing smirk graced her face with the last words.

Elizabeth and Jane moved towards the ballroom as Mary herded the younger girls behind them. At the door to the ballroom, Darcy greeted the sisters.

"How nice you look this evening. I hope each of you will save me a dance."

The younger girls giggled and nodded, while a red-faced Mary said, "If you wish, Mr. Darcy." Most of Darcy's dance card was filled by Elizabeth and her sisters, as well as his own sister. A dance with Mrs. Hurst and Miss Bingley and the final set with Elizabeth would fill his dance card. It would be the most he had danced at any ball.

When everyone but Elizabeth moved into the ballroom, Darcy offered his arm to his betrothed. "You look beautiful this evening, my dear."

"I thank you for my lovely gift." A short time before the Bennets departed from Longbourn, a servant in the Darcy livery had delivered a box for Elizabeth. When she opened it, she found that it contained a dozen small white rosebuds. Enclosed was a sweet note from her betrothed.

*Elizabeth,*

    *I thought these would look lovely in your beautiful dark hair.*

*Affectionately,*
*William*

"You are most welcome. I must admit to being a bit jealous. Those little buds get to caress your rich tresses, something I have longed to do." A shy smile appeared on her face, though Elizabeth blushed at his words. "How do you like your replacement dress?" Darcy's sly smile made Elizabeth wonder if there was more to his question.

"I love it. I do not know who gave Mrs. Harris the instructions for the gown. I expected that Papa would send me into the shop to order the new dress, but I never heard mention of it." As his smile grew, Elizabeth tilted her head to the side and studied Darcy. "William, did you have anything to do with my dress?"

"What do you mean?" His tone was innocent.

"Did you pick out this dress?"

"I may have had some say in the choices."

"What do you mean?"

"Well, thanks to your father's distraction with his book, he allowed me to write the note to the seamstress. I thought this color would be extremely suited to you, and I suspected that you preferred elegant simplicity to excessive frills. I am delighted I was correct, for I look forward to showering you with gifts for the remainder of our lives."

"William, I do not need gifts. All I need to make me happy is you."

"That may be true, but you will have to learn to accept them. You can ask Georgiana; I enjoy surprising those I love with special gifts."

"Where is Georgiana?"

"She is seated just over there. Shall we join her?"

At Elizabeth's nod, they made their way to Georgiana and Mrs. Annesley.

"Good evening, Georgiana. You look beautiful."

"Thank you, Lizzy. You look beautiful, as well. Your dress is exquisite."

"Thank you." Elizabeth and Darcy exchanged a smile filled with a meaning Georgiana did not understand. When the music began, Darcy bowed and escorted Elizabeth to the dance floor. They did not speak as they moved through the first dance, but their eyes and their touches said more than words ever could. Laughter and conversation continued through the second dance of the set.

Their behavior caused a great deal of gossip behind the fans of the matrons that evening.

Darcy danced next with Georgiana, then danced the sets promised to Miss Bingley and to Jane. Between sets, he and Elizabeth were always together, often with Georgiana or one of Elizabeth's sisters. As the supper set began, Darcy had Elizabeth back in his arms. While they danced, they spoke of their future, discussing their hopes and dreams. When the set ended, they retrieved Georgiana from her seat and moved into the dining room. They were seated at the main table near Jane and Bingley. Mr. and Mrs. Bennet sat at the other end of the same table near the Hursts and Miss Bingley.

Once everyone was seated, Bingley stood and addressed his guests. "I would like to welcome you all to Netherfield Park and express my gratitude for the warm welcome we received to your neighborhood. I hope you will enjoy yourselves this evening. Before we serve the dinner, Mr. Bennet has an announcement he would like to make."

As Bingley sat down, a murmur spread through the crowd, speculating at the forthcoming announcement, Mr. Bennet stood and said, "It gives me the greatest pleasure to announce the engagement of my daughter Elizabeth to Mr. Fitzwilliam Darcy of Pemberley in Derbyshire. They are to marry in early January." Loud applause and calls of congratulations followed the announcement.

Bingley stood again, saying, "Please raise your glasses and join me in a toast to Mr. Darcy and Miss Elizabeth." He paused as the company raised their glasses. "May you have a long and happy life together." Darcy and Elizabeth smiled at each other as they clinked their glasses and drank in acknowledgment of the toast in their honor. When Mr. Bingley sat down, an army of footmen began serving the white soup. The dinner had started.

The room buzzed with pleasant conversation as the residents of Meryton enjoyed the superb supper prepared by the Bingleys' chef. After dinner, several of the local ladies entertained. Elizabeth sang a duet to the accompaniment of Mary and Georgiana.

Throughout the dinner and entertainment, Miss Bingley kept up her pleasant façade. When everyone returned to the ballroom, she lingered until she and the servants were the only ones in the room. Crossing the hallway, Caroline glanced about, then turned away from the ballroom and down a corridor towards the back of the house. She opened a door onto the terrace. A tall man dressed entirely in black slipped inside.

Caroline put a finger to her lips to indicate the need for silence. She led the man back the way she had come and paused before a closed door. The gentleman slipped inside the darkened room, lit only by the fire burning in the grate.

"Remain here and stay quiet. I will be back as soon as I can." At his nod, Caroline exited, closing the door behind her. The man slipped off his coat and took a seat in the chair behind the door to wait.

# MISS BINGLEY'S SCHEME GOES AWRY

SURPRISINGLY, LYDIA DID NOT HAVE A partner for the first set after supper. After watching the dancing for a moment or two, she decided to go to the ladies' retiring room. When she reached the doorway to the ballroom, she noticed Miss Bingley looking furtively around the hall. Curious, Lydia followed Caroline as the latter disappeared down a long hallway. When the woman reached a doorway, she opened it and a man in black stepped inside. Lydia slipped into a dark alcove as the couple turned and walked back the way Miss Bingley had come. Lydia pressed herself tighter against the wall as they passed her hiding place.

When they turned the corner, Lydia rushed from the alcove to follow. Peeking carefully around the corner, she saw them pause before a door. As the door opened, the light from within reflected on the man's face. Gasping in surprise, Lydia hurriedly ducked out of sight and put her hand over her mouth to stifle any further sound. She listened for any noise that would indicate the others were coming towards her, but she heard nothing. She dared not look around the corner for fear of discovery, though she placed her ear as close to the edge as possible, straining to hear anything.

Snatches of conversation in Miss Bingley's quiet voice reached her. "Remain here. . .quiet. . .back. . .soon. . .Remember. . . you must . . ."

Lydia was shocked into stillness as the sound of footsteps receded. What was he doing

219

here and what did Miss Bingley's words mean? With unusual clarity, the memory of a discussion with her sisters came rushing back. That memory sparked her into action.

Returning to the ballroom, Lydia found Kitty. Taking her hand, she pulled her sister along until they also found Mary. Grabbing Mary by the hand, Lydia dragged her sisters after her until they reached a small anteroom. In the farthest corner of the room, she related to them what she had seen and heard. Her sisters were as shocked as she was.

"This is what I think we should do." Lydia began outlining her rapidly developed plan. When she was through, her sisters looked at her, smiles on their faces.

"What if we are dancing when it happens?"

Lydia thought for a moment. "Pretend to be faint and ask your partner to accompany you to the hall."

Everyone agreed to the plan. One at a time, the three sisters slipped back into the ballroom.

Caroline Bingley wandered the edges of the ballroom, surveying the proceedings and speaking to the occasional guest. Elizabeth was scheduled to dance the last dance with Mr. Darcy, so she would need to strike before then.

At the end of the set, Caroline located Jane and escorted her to the hallway. "Forgive me for disturbing you, but I thought you would wish to know that I observed Miss Elizabeth going upstairs to the ladies' withdrawing room. She was looking a little pale."

"Thank you, Miss Bingley. Would you please tell Mr. Bingley I will return soon?"

"Of course."

Jane ascended the staircase. Caroline watched with a satisfied smile. Returning to the ballroom, she looked for her true prey. The set for the penultimate dance of the evening was about to form. Caroline scanned the crowd and discovered Elizabeth's partner taking her to the floor. Hurrying in their direction, Caroline arrived just before they joined the set.

"Miss Elizabeth, pray forgive me, but Miss Bennet felt unwell. I took her somewhere she might rest and said that I would fetch you to attend her."

"Please excuse me, Captain Carter."

"Of course, Miss Elizabeth. Please let me know if I can be of assistance."

"Thank you, Captain. Perhaps you would find my sister Mary."

"It would be my pleasure." Captain Carter was a tall man. He turned about until he spotted Mary and then moved in her direction as Elizabeth followed Miss Bingley from the room.

Kitty and Lydia were lurking near the entrance to the ballroom and saw Miss Bingley and Elizabeth heading in their direction. After they passed, the girls followed them down the hallway, quiet as mice.

Meanwhile, Captain Carter approached Mary. After explaining what had occurred, Mary asked that he hurry to find Mr. Bingley and Mr. Darcy, then send them to the hallway. She rushed away.

Captain Carter was surprised by the usually calm Miss Mary's behavior but did as she requested.

Lydia and Kitty stepped into the hallway to see Elizabeth and Miss Bingley before the door where the man in black waited. Whispering into Kitty's ear, the two young ladies rushed forward, their dancing shoes making almost no sound. The door opened. Running ahead, Kitty pushed Elizabeth to the side before she could enter the room. She shoved with such force that her sister landed on the ground. Lydia now stood behind Miss Bingley and pushed her through the open door. Then she grabbed the door handle and swung the door closed. Kitty joined her. They held on tightly to prevent it from being opened. When she arrived, Mary added her slight weight to the effort.

Everything had happened very quickly and those involved were too surprised to speak. That did not last long, as a cacophony of voices soon spoke at once.

"Lydia, Kitty, what are you doing?" asked a startled Elizabeth from her seat on the floor.

"Elizabeth, are you well?" came Darcy's worried voice as he moved to assist her in rising.

After a long pause and what sounded like a slap, Miss Bingley's voice called out to be released as she banged on the door.

It was upon this scene of chaos that Mr. Bingley arrived.

"What in heaven's name is going on?"

Elizabeth and Darcy had no answer to that question. Mary and Kitty looked to Lydia to answer, as she was the only one, besides Miss Bingley, involved from the beginning. Lydia began her tale of having observed Miss Bingley's strange actions and of Miss Bingley having let someone in the room. "I believe she lured Lizzy here for the purpose of having her compromised. I think you will agree when you learn who is in there! By the way, after we closed the door, there was a long silence and the sound of a slap." A broad grin covered Lydia's face.

Bingley stepped before the door and the three sisters let go. Behind them stood Darcy and Elizabeth, his arm around her waist, pulling her close to his side. The door swung open.

Everyone in the hallway gasped at the sight before them. There stood a scarlet-faced Caroline Bingley. The front of her dress appeared torn from the shoulder, and she clutched it to her chest. Her lips were red and swollen, and much of her hair tumbled around her. Over her shoulder could be seen the face of Mr. Collins.

"Caroline, what have you been doing?"

"I was attacked."

"How did Mr. Collins get here? He was definitely not invited!"

"Indeed, I was. Miss Bingley sent a letter inviting me," came the pompous reply.

"Caroline, how could you correspond with a man to whom you are not engaged? Well, between that and your appearance, you are well and truly compromised. I will expect you to present yourself to me in the morning, sir, to discuss the marriage settlement."

"But I do not wish to marry Miss Bingley. I came to marry my cousin, Elizabeth. If Lady Catherine supported my claim to you as I expected, I would not have had to resort to this."

"Why on earth would you think I would accept you now when I refused you before?" cried Elizabeth. "I detest you!"

"Mr. Collins, as my aunt gave my relationship with Miss Elizabeth her blessing, I doubt she will be pleased when she learns of your behavior this night. She cannot revoke the living, but you might wish she could as living with a disgruntled Lady Catherine is anything but pleasant. As for you, Miss Bingley, when we spoke, you accepted the fact that I would never ask for your hand in marriage," Darcy said. "Why, then, would you arrange to have Miss Elizabeth compromised?"

"I could not accept that I was not worthy to be Mrs. Darcy while this country nobody was. It isn't fair. If I cannot have you, neither can she!"

"You have no say in whom I marry and your actions guarantee I will not see you again in the future under any circumstances." With that, Darcy turned and led Elizabeth away. Her sisters followed her and they all returned to the ballroom. They met Jane at the bottom of the stairs.

"There you are, Lizzy. I was worried about you. Caroline said you went to the ladies' withdrawing room and that you were unwell. How did you get here?"

"It is a long story, Jane. I will tell you everything tomorrow."

Darcy offered his other arm to Jane. "Bingley must attend to a household matter. Will you not join us until he returns?"

Jane accepted the arm offered to her and accompanied the others to the ballroom, though she looked in confusion at her sisters trailing them.

Watching the others walk away, Bingley pushed his sister back into the room and closed the door behind him.

"How could you do such a thing, Caroline? What makes you think you have the right to decide whom someone can or cannot love? If you had just accepted his words and left things alone, you would have always been welcome as a part of his circle. Darcy began to relax around you after you two spoke. Now, you have guaranteed that you will never achieve your goal of being part of the first circle of society. You will see him only from afar when he visits his aunt at Rosings Park."

"I am not going to Rosings Park."

"Indeed, you are. You and Mr. Collins will marry as soon as I can arrange it."

"As I said, I do not wish to marry Miss Bingley."

"You compromised her and you will marry her or I will report your action to the church. Though her behavior sometimes leaves something to be desired, she is attractive and has a dowry of twenty thousand pounds."

Collins' eyes lit up at the size of her dowry. "You are correct, Mr. Bingley. I will do my duty."

"Now you will find yourself a room at the inn in Meryton and report to me first thing tomorrow morning. Remember, I do know where to find you should you fail to appear," Bingley said sternly. "You, Caroline, will go to your room and remain there until morning. If you do anything other than what I tell you, I will cut off your allowance and send you to our relatives in York to live in disgrace."

"But, Charles. . ." she began.

"No buts, Caroline." He took his sister by the arm and stepped into the hallway, where he motioned to a nearby footman. "Please escort Miss Bingley to her room and remain outside her door. She is not feeling well. Do not allow anyone to bother her and do not allow her to exit."

"Yes, sir." Bingley watched as they mounted the stairs. With a shake of his head, he turned towards the ballroom. Bingley arrived as the music for the final set started. Glancing about, he found Jane standing with Darcy and Miss Elizabeth. After making his way across the room, he bowed to Jane and said, "I believe this is our dance."

Jane placed her hand in his and the two couples took to the dance floor. Bingley had planned a waltz for the final set. With broad smiles, the men took the women they loved in their arms and twirled them around the dance floor. Darcy and Bingley were slow to release Jane and Elizabeth from their arms. Darcy and Elizabeth stood holding hands and staring at each other. However, at Elizabeth's gasp, Darcy turned to see the cause.

Bingley was still holding Jane Bennet's hands as well. He was down on one knee before her in the middle of the ballroom floor.

"My dear, sweet Miss Bennet, I can wait no longer. I must beg you to accept my hand in marriage. Having you here in my home on this special night, at this special time of year, I want nothing more than to spend Christmas with you now and forever."

A blushing Jane, with tears spilling from her eyes, took a deep breath and nodded before finding her voice. "I would be delighted to accept, and I would like nothing better than to spend the rest of my life with you."

The guests burst forth with best wishes and exclamations of delight. Elizabeth rushed into her sister's arms. "Oh, Jane. I am so happy for you. Is it not wonderful that we both found good men to love and who love us in return? It is even better that they are best friends, for it means we will often be together in the years to come."

Darcy clapped his friend's back as Elizabeth spoke with Jane. "Congratulations, Charles. I hope you two will be very happy. Perhaps you should look for an estate close to Pemberley, as I am sure Elizabeth would love to have her dearest sister living nearby."

There was no chance for them to say more, for by that time Mr. and Mrs. Bennet arrived to offer their congratulations.

"Oh, my dear, Jane. I knew how it would be. I knew you could not be so beautiful for nothing."

"Congratulations, Jane," said her father as he kissed her cheek. Extending his hand to Bingley, he said, "Congratulations, young man. I hope you realize how dear my Jane is and will care for her as she deserves."

"You can count on it, sir."

Bingley escorted Jane to the door with him to farewell their guests. After the last one departed, the Bennet carriage pulled to the door. Mr. and Mrs. Bennet and the younger girls exited the house and Mr. Bennet helped the ladies into the carriage. Standing on opposite sides of the hall, with the open door providing privacy, each gentleman took his ladylove into his arms and bestowed a gentle kiss which gradually grew in intensity. The sound of Mr. Bennet clearing his throat from just beyond the door returned the two couples to their senses. Each man tucked his lady's arm in his and led her to the family carriage.

Darcy helped Elizabeth into the carriage and kissed her hand before releasing it. "Until tomorrow, dearest, loveliest Elizabeth," he breathed as he released her fingers.

Bingley replaced him and handed Jane into the vehicle. Repeating his friend's actions, he whispered, "Until tomorrow, my angel," before releasing Jane's hand. The gentlemen remained until the carriage turned out of the drive. Then they retired to Bingley's study for a brandy before retiring for the night.

# SHARING CHRISTMAS

IN THE DAYS FOLLOWING THE DEPARTURE of the newlywed Collinses, things settled into a pattern. The ladies of Longbourn and Georgiana spent each morning in planning the upcoming double wedding of Jane and Bingley and Elizabeth and Darcy. Georgiana was thrilled to be included in the planning and activities. Her relationship with Elizabeth grew ever closer. Georgiana's genteel behavior and good sense rubbed off on Kitty and Lydia. Mary also became less rigid and moralistic in her behavior. Georgiana even convinced her to read a novel, which they delighted in discussing together. The Bennet sisters' more outgoing personalities also helped Georgiana to overcome her extreme shyness.

The gentlemen would arrive an hour before teatime, so the couples could walk or sit on opposite sides of the small back parlor, where they could chaperone one another while still enjoying a modicum of privacy to talk. Sometimes they would sit together and play cards or make plans for spending time together in the future.

On Christmas Eve, the families gathered for dinner at Netherfield Park before attending the midnight service. The next day, the families again gathered, this time at Longbourn, to celebrate Christmas. Shortly after breakfast, the Netherfield party arrived. They gathered in the parlor and everyone took a seat. Kitty, Lydia, and Georgiana handed out the gifts—a task they completed with great excitement as a footman accompanied the

Netherfield guests carrying gifts. Two trips were required to bring them all in the house. The Gardiner family was also present, and the children's excitement at the sight of so many presents had them trembling with joy.

Mr. Bingley used his ties to trade and provided each of the four younger Bennet ladies with several yards of floral patterned cotton for a new day dress. Both Mrs. Bennet and Miss Bennet received a quantity of silk for a gown. Jane's was a beautiful sapphire blue that matched her lovely eyes. On top of the cut fabric sat a small black velvet box. Jane opened it to find a heart-shaped sapphire surrounded by diamonds and suspended from a delicate silver chain.

"My mother possesses a set of diamonds that my father gave to her upon their marriage. It is the only piece of the Bingley family jewels. I wanted you to have something just for you that we can add to the collection. I chose the sapphires to match your eyes and your engagement ring." Jane thanked him tenderly, her eyes shining with unshed tears. Mrs. Bennet commented profusely about the expensive jewels, but Mr. Bennet shushed her to open his gift from Bingley. It revealed a box of expensive imported cigars.

Mr. and Mrs. Gardiner received gifts similar to Mr. and Mrs. Bennet and each of the young Gardiners received a toy. The Darcys purchased bonnets for Mary, Kitty, and Lydia, in colors that matched the fabric from Bingley. Mrs. Bennet and Miss Bennet received soft cashmere shawls to complement their fabrics. Mr. Bennet received two first edition books. Mr. and Mrs. Gardiner received two tickets to an exclusive concert scheduled at Drury Lane Theater. The two

Gardiner boys each received a set of toy soldiers in different-colored uniforms so they could battle each other. The older Gardiner daughter received a porcelain tea set with delicate flowers painted on it, while the younger daughter received a lovely doll with a porcelain head and curls the same color as her own.

Elizabeth was the last to open her gift from the Darcys. Her box contained a length of lovely amber silk. She also had a black velvet box on top of the fabric, though hers was much larger than Jane's. She opened it to reveal a magnificent set of jewels containing a necklace, a bracelet, a ring, and earbobs. Taking in the surprising sight, Elizabeth could not help the small gasp that escaped.

Darcy, who was watching her closely, smiled at her surprise and delight. "Do you like it, Elizabeth?" he whispered.

"It is the most beautiful thing I have ever seen, William. Is it part of the Darcy family jewels?"

"No, I bought this just for you. The color reminds me of the specks that appear in your sparkling eyes. They are like rays of sunshine that make them light up even more than your bubbling personality does. I find them mesmerizing."

"Thank you, William. I will cherish them as I do your words."

"What did you get, Lizzy?" demanded her mother.

Elizabeth lifted the swatch of fabric from the box to show it to the others. Dropping it, she then lifted the jewelry box and turned it to face the others.

The box contained a choker with three strands of pearls. Both sides held a square topaz surrounded by diamonds that connected the strands. In the front, each strand was slightly longer than the one above it. Suspended from the longest string of pearls was a larger square topaz, also surrounded by diamonds. The bracelet was similar, with a diamond-surrounded topaz on top. The ring was diamond and topaz, and the earbobs held the diamond-encrusted topaz suspended from a large pearl by a diamond chain. A brilliant gold setting held the stones.

"Oh my stars!" cried Mrs. Bennet. "I have never seen anything so dazzling!"

"It is quite lovely," agreed Mrs. Gardiner.

"Can I borrow it, Lizzy?" asked Lydia. Elizabeth shook her head at her youngest sister and barely refrained from rolling her eyes.

The children played with the toys as the adults talked. When Mrs. Hill announced dinner, the family sat down to a feast. The five-course meal included roast beef, roast goose, venison, pheasant, and a fish dish. There were roasted potatoes, Brussel sprouts, and carrots, apples, and onions seasoned with sage and nutmeg, as well as baked squash sweetened with cinnamon and brown sugar. There were Yorkshire pudding and other assorted breads with black butter and jams. The dessert course included a flaming plum pudding, whipped syllabub, fruit, cheese, nuts, candies, and sweetmeats.

After dinner, many of the adults dozed off, giving the young people time to themselves. When they awoke, Mary played several Christmas carols on the pianoforte before the group enjoyed games of charades and snapdragon.

All agreed that it was a wonderful day. The young couples were delighted that their weddings were just over a week away.

# FINDING HAPPILY EVER AFTER

The January morning glistened in the sunshine. The previous day had begun with rain before the temperature had dropped and changed the precipitation to snow. On her wedding day, Elizabeth woke with the sun. She sat on the window seat in her bedroom to watch it rise. As the sun soared higher in the sky, the snow changed from orange to peach to pink before it became a blinding white world. The trees sparkled like diamonds, their bare branches coated in ice. A downy white fluff blanketed the landscape as far as the eye could see.

Soon, Elizabeth detected footsteps traipsing along the hallway. They were heavy and slow as they passed her door the first time. However, on the return trip, they sounded quick and light. Realizing that they must be filling the tub, Elizabeth gathered her things and quietly exited the room. As her hair was much thicker than Jane's and her elder sister was not a morning person, Elizabeth would be the first to bathe and wash her hair in preparation for her wedding.

Elizabeth sank into the hot, lavender-scented water of the half-filled hipbath. Fortunately, a fire blazed in the large fireplace in the bathing room. Sally, the maid she shared with her sisters, made quick work of washing Elizabeth's hair before leaving her to soak for a few minutes. When she returned with two more buckets, Sally set them on the hearth to stay warm before handing Elizabeth a bar of scented soap. Elizabeth quickly washed. Then Sally poured one of the buckets over her head to rinse her hair. Elizabeth stood as the other bucket was used to rinse her body. Sally handed her a towel from the rack before the fire, and Elizabeth wrapped it tightly around her. Sally then gave her a second towel, which Elizabeth wrapped around her long locks. She twisted it on top of her head before slipping down the hall to her room.

There, Elizabeth sat before the fire that the maid had built up while she bathed. After unwrapping her hair, Elizabeth reached for her comb and began to pull it through her tangled tresses. When detangled, she pushed her hair behind her shoulders and turned her back to the fire to allow it to dry.

Jane awoke to the sight of Elizabeth's head bent over a letter. She wore a brilliant smile, but Jane also spotted tears on her cheek.

"Are you well, Lizzy?" came Jane's sleepy voice.

Brushing at the tears on her face, Elizabeth looked up at Jane, her smile still in place. "I am well, Jane, but I cannot believe my good fortune in finding a man like William. He is everything I ever dreamed of and more."

"I feel equally blessed," replied a dreamy-eyed Jane.

"I believe your water is ready and I suggest that you hurry or Lydia may try to sneak in ahead of you." The sisters laughed, knowing that Lizzy's words were entirely true. Lydia, being the youngest, often had the last use of the tub that the sisters shared. In many households, the entire family used the same water. Mrs. Bennet did not subscribe to that belief, so everyone had fresh water for bathing, but it was only a few inches, as it would have taken most of the day to warm enough water to fill the tub for seven family members.

Lizzy, Jane, hurry. It is time to leave for the church," Mrs. Bennet called up the stairs. Mrs. Gardiner and Mrs. Hill had kindly kept Mrs. Bennet busy throughout the morning, allowing the girls a quiet, peaceful time during which to prepare for the biggest day of their lives.

"The girls are ready, Mrs. Bennet. You should go on to the church. We will be only a few minutes behind you."

Seeing Jane as she reached the bottom of the stairs, Mrs. Bennet said, "Oh," adding with a sniff, "My mother's pearl combs look so beautiful in your hair." The Bennet matriarch had presented them to Jane the evening before.

As Sally put the finishing touches on Elizabeth's hair, a knock came at the door. "Come in, Papa."

Jane had already descended the stairs on her father's arm, so Lizzy knew it was Mr. Bennet coming back to accompany her. Mr. Bennet stepped into the room but stopped in his tracks at the sight of his favorite daughter. "Lizzy, my dear girl. You look wonderful."

"Thank you, Papa."

Catching her eyes in the mirror of her dressing table, her father said, "As you know, we named you after my dear mother." Elizabeth nodded. "She gave me something to give you on your wedding day." Mr. Bennet handed her a small box.

Lifting the lid, Elizabeth gasped, "Papa, these are beautiful." Inside, on a bed of velvet, sat a pair of large pearls surrounded by diamonds with a matching pendant. Sally took the box and Mr. Bennet removed the necklace, which he placed around Elizabeth's neck. Sally set the box on the dressing table and lifted the earbobs, then put them in Elizabeth's ears. The maid placed her bonnet on her head and Mr. Bennet held out his hand to assist Elizabeth in rising. They joined Jane in the hall and the three of them descended the stairs, stepped into the waiting carriage, and took the short ride to the Meryton church.

With a last wave to her family, Elizabeth Darcy settled into the seat across from her husband as the carriage pulled away from Longbourn, taking Elizabeth to her new London home. Staring at her, Elizabeth's husband of about five hours, Fitzwilliam Darcy, wasted no time before moving to settle himself beside his new bride. He removed her hat and gloves, tossing them onto the rear-facing seat. When her wedding bonnet was out of the way, Darcy cupped his beautiful wife's face in his hands before gently caressing her lips with his. The kiss began tenderly, but grew in intensity, each trying to show the other their love and desire. When they finally drew apart, they were both gasping for breath, their hearts racing. Elizabeth snuggled into her husband's embrace, her head on his chest, listening to his heartbeat slow.

"For all her excitability, your mother does set an excellent table. The wedding breakfast was a lovely affair."

"Did you tell Mama that?" asked his wife with a cheeky grin.

"I thought I might just send her a note." Darcy would not meet his wife's eye, but her tinkling laugh caused his chest to begin shaking. Soon his deep rumble could also be heard. Their conversation continued, ranging from topic to topic. They spoke of everything and nothing, talking of their hopes and dreams.

When the carriage pulled up in front of Darcy House, Elizabeth was surprised to see the servants lined up to greet her. As she stepped down from the carriage, Darcy swept her in his arms and carried her up the front steps to the cheers of the servants. This auspicious beginning was just the start of the Darcys' happily ever after.

# EPILOGUE

FOR THOSE OF YOU WONDERING WHAT became of Mr. Collins and his new wife, the former Miss Bingley, they returned to Rosings immediately following their wedding. However, before their arrival, Lady Catherine received a letter from her nephew thanking her for her good wishes and understanding of his and Anne's feelings about marrying each other. He also included the information about her parson's failed attempt to compromise Darcy's betrothed. He gave her all the particulars of the incident. As the great lady read the letter, her anger mounted.

When Mr. Collins returned to his home, he wasted no time in sending word to Lady Catherine and requesting the opportunity to present his new bride. He was thrilled to receive her reply for an immediate interview.

The butler's solemn voice intoned, "Mr. and Mrs. Collins, ma'am."

"Lady Catherine, how grateful we are that you would deign to receive us so soon after our return. Allow me to present my bride, Mrs. Caroline Collins nee Bingley."

Caroline barely dipped a curtsey and was quickly chastised by her husband. "My dear, I am sure you recognize that my dear patroness is far above both of us in society and is due all courtesies related to her." His tone was quite firm, as he feared angering Lady Catherine further.

Caroline glared at her spouse before offering a deeper curtsey. "It is a pleasure to meet you, Lady Catherine. I am well acquainted with your nephew, Mr. Darcy. Our families have been quite close for about four years now. I should warn you, my lady, that Mr. Darcy has fallen for a fortune-hunter. She is a nobody, a country chit who will disgrace him in society."

"And you are the disgraced daughter of a tradesman. How dare you accuse my nephew of such ridiculous behavior. You are merely spouting sour grapes, as you desired to be the next mistress of Pemberley. Darcy would never have married the bitter, conniving daughter of a tradesman above the daughter of a gentleman." The lady turned to her parson. "And you, Mr. Collins. How dare you go against my wishes and try to steal my nephew's betrothed. I am very displeased, Mr. Collins, very displeased."

The rotund parson cowered before his patroness, bowing so low that he nearly toppled over in an undignified heap. "I am sorry, Lady Catherine. The last I knew, you were unhappy with your nephew. I thought I was helping you, as I always wish to do, my lady."

"I am disappointed in both of you. Do not present yourselves before me until I send for you. Nor should you expect to receive any invitations for quite some time. I am most seriously displeased."

Lady Catherine never did forgive her parson nor take to his ambitious, manipulative wife. Over the next seven years of service at Hunsford, Mr. Collins struggled under the weight of Lady Catherine's displeasure. It slowly wore him down until he refused to eat and eventually died before he could inherit Longbourn. His wife had denied him her bed throughout their marriage, so there was no son to inherit in his place. Because of her behavior at the Netherfield ball, Caroline never contacted her family for the remainder of her life. She used what remained of her dowry and set herself up in the best London neighborhood she could afford. She attempted to contact friends from school, but too many years had passed and no one was interested in renewing the acquaintance after learning of her lowly marriage. Caroline remained a lonely, bitter, condescending woman to the end of her days.

# ACKNOWLEDGMENTS

THANKS TO MY AMAZING SISTER-IN-law, Lori Whitlock, for making the cover template and teaching me how to make this cover and future ones. I am also grateful to Tonya Blust for her work editing the book.

# AUTHOR BIOGRAPHY

Linda C. Thompson has had a forty-five-year love affair with Pride and Prejudice in particularly and the Regency Era in general. She cannot get enough of the love story between Fitzwilliam Darcy and Elizabeth Bennet. This love affair has led her to author seven books, which reimagine the love story between Darcy and Elizabeth.

Linda's husband of 31 years is the Elizabeth in their relationship. Linda is the shy, formal one and uses her writing as an outlet for her romantic nature.

Hearing from fans is one of her biggest joys. You can keep in touch with the author in the following ways:

Email: lindathompson.author@gmail.com
Facebook: Linda Thompson Books page
Instagram: Lindasusancooperthompson
Twitter: @LindyT07
Website: lindacthompsonbooks.com

# OTHER BOOKS BY
# LINDA C. THOMPSON

## HER UNFORGETTABLE LAUGH
Her Unforgettable Laugh Series, Book 1
A Pride and Prejudice Variation

Dark curls and an unforgettably sweet laugh are all he knows of his sister's rescuer. Later, a second glimpse shows her to be lovely, and he hears her melodious laugh again. Darcy wonders what it would be like to meet this remarkable—and remarkably lovely—young woman. Would the spirit that compelled her to assist a stranger bring some joy into his lonely life? Would they ever meet? Or will he always be left wondering?

Little does Fitzwilliam Darcy know that his trip to Hertfordshire will bring him face to face with the lovely young woman whose unforgettable laugh has haunted his dreams for the last several years. Will she be anything like the woman he has built up in his dreams? Will he be able to avoid Miss Bingley long enough to discover more about this mysterious young woman?

## Laughter Through Trials
Her Unforgettable Laugh Series, Book 2
A Pride and Prejudice Variation

Dark curls and an unforgettably sweet laugh . . .

In Book 1 of the Her Unforgettable Laugh series, a trip to Hertfordshire brought Fitzwilliam Darcy face to face with the woman who had haunted his dreams for five years. Their chance meeting led to a courtship, despite the efforts of those who wished to separate them. Now Elizabeth Bennet is traveling to London, where she will be introduced to Darcy's family and the ton. How will Elizabeth be received? Will their love flourish and grow? Or will new trials overwhelm them?

# THE LAUGHTER OF LOVE
Her Unforgettable Laugh Series, Book 3
A Pride and Prejudice Variation

Dark curls and an unforgettably sweet laugh . . .

In Book 2 of the Her Unforgettable Laugh series, Darcy and Elizabeth celebrated their courtship as Elizabeth was introduced to the Fitzwilliam family and London society. Their sojourn in town presented a few difficulties. However, the strength of their love allowed them to face their challenges and outwit their enemies.

Now Darcy and Elizabeth are returning to Hertfordshire for their wedding. Elizabeth worries about the one trial they have yet to face: Mrs. Bennet. Her mother refuses to prepare the simple, elegant affair the couple wishes for their wedding day. Will it be the day of their dreams ... or a disaster?

Ultimately, the wedding turns out and Darcy and Elizabeth are excited to begin their life together. The bright future before them fills their hearts with joy. Both know that they will face periods of contentment and heartache; however, united, they will confront whatever comes their way. Will those whom they have previously encountered allow them to enjoy their happiness? Or must they overcome more misfortune?

## THE COMPANION'S SECRET
A Pride and Prejudice Variation

"You must marry her," the stern voice said. "I need to gain control of her inheritance before she reaches her next birthday. It need not be a long marriage, but marry her you must."

Alone in the world, Elizabeth Bennet has had to rely upon herself. She knows that escape is the only way to ensure her safety. With the help of Longbourn's faithful servants, Elizabeth disappears from her home and the odious heir. She is determined to find a way to support herself and remain hidden until after her birthday.

Fortune smiles on Elizabeth when a series of events offers her the role of companion to Georgiana Darcy. Despite her position, Elizabeth finds herself attracted to her new employer. Can he ever see her as more than his sister's companion? Sometimes, Elizabeth thinks that Mr. Darcy cares for her, too. Yet will his attraction—if that is, indeed, what he feels—survive when he learns the truth about her?

Hidden away at Pemberley, will Elizabeth be able to safely conceal herself until she comes of age? What surprises does the future hold in store for her?

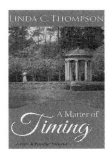

## A MATTER OF TIMING
A Pride and Prejudice Variation

They say that timing is everything . . .

Their chance meeting at Pemberley helps Elizabeth Bennet realize her true feelings for Mr. Darcy. That same meeting gives him the opportunity to show Elizabeth that he has taken her criticism to heart and made improvements to his behavior. Will this new start finally lead to their happily ever after?

How might the relationship between Elizabeth and Darcy have been different if they had become betrothed before Elizabeth learned of Lydia's elopement? Would they have traveled to London together? Would Elizabeth have helped with her sister's recovery? Would Lydia and Wickham still have married? Or would Elizabeth have found another way to save her youngest sister?

A Matter of Timing answers all these questions and more.

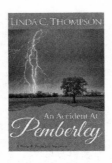

## AN ACCIDENT AT PEMBERLEY
A Pride and Prejudice Variation

In the time before Mr. Bingley takes up residence at Netherfield Park, Elizabeth travels into Derbyshire with her Aunt and Uncle Gardiner. One day, as her friends and relations visit with some of Mrs. Gardiner's childhood friends, Elizabeth explores the small village. Without realizing it, she strays farther and farther from the village, unconsciously walking in the direction of Pemberley, the estate that the group had visited two days prior.

Lost in her thoughts and the beauty of the Derbyshire countryside, Elizabeth fails to notice the storm clouds building above her. At the first flash of lightning and peal of thunder, she seeks shelter from the storm, Rushing for a dense tree line where she might avoid the impending rain, Elizabeth Bennet meets with a dreadful accident.

Returning from business in London, Fitzwilliam Darcy races across the grounds of Pemberley, trying to outrun the storm. After coming across a beautiful young woman who has been injured, he takes her home so that his staff can care for her. Darcy hopes her presence will help lift his mother's melancholy.

When Elizabeth regains consciousness, she has no memory of her name or her past. During the many weeks of her recovery, Elizabeth grows close to Mr. Darcy and his mother, Lady Anne. When Elizabeth recovers enough to leave the estate, the Darcys decide that she needs an identity that will protect her from gossip. And so, Miss Elizabeth Chamberlayne, a long-lost Darcy cousin, is born. After receiving two requests, Darcy accepts an invitation to stay with his friend, Mr. Bingley, at Netherfield Park. The ladies will join him.

What will happen when Elizabeth comes face to face with her family? Will she remember them? Or will her memory still be a blank? All the original characters in Jane Austen's *Pride and Prejudice* make an appearance. How will Elizabeth's lack of memory affect her interactions with them?